I still didn't know what they wanted from me but I knew I was about to find out. When Reser finally told me, I said nothing doing. I don't know what I'd expected but it was nothing like that. I said I'd rather go back to jail. And I meant it. But all the time I was talking tough, when I was away from the hotel, they went back there and picked up Thelma. So I had my choice: Thelma alive or Thelma dead. It wasn't any choice at all and they knew it. If I didn't kill Whittaker, they'd kill my wife.

Also available in Star

DEBT OF HONOUR

THE DOMINO VENDETTA

Adam Kennedy

A STAR BOOK
published by
the Paperback Division of
W. H. ALLEN & Co. Ltd

A Star Book
Published in 1983
by the Paperback Division of
W. H. Allen & Co. Ltd
A Howard and Wyndham Company
44 Hill Street, London W1X 8LB

First published in Great Britain by
W. H. Allen & Co. Ltd, 1982

Reproduced, printed and bound in Great Britain by
Hazell Watson & Viney Ltd, Aylesbury, Bucks

ISBN 0 352 31314 5

He who kills a man shall be put to death . . . as he has done it shall be done to him, fracture for fracture, eye for eye, tooth for tooth; as he has disfigured a man, he shall be disfigured . . . and he who kills a man shall be put to death.

Leviticus 24.17–21

This book is dedicated to
my splendid sons . . .
Jack and Regan

PART ONE

CHAPTER ONE

FIVE DAYS AFTER they killed his wife, after they ran Thelma down, crushed her against a wall on the road winding into the village, five days later they came to kill him.

Tucker stood on the upper terrace of the house they'd found for him in Costa Rica, overlooking the ocean, seven miles downcoast from Puntarenas, and watched the grey sedan pull in off the access road and stop in the shaded parking area at the bottom of the outside staircase. Ross Pine got out on one side of the car and the man they called Brookshire got out on the driver's side.

Tucker waited silently at the top of the stairs, watched them start to climb the steps, talking quietly together. When they looked up and saw him, he raised the rifle and fired, aiming low.

He shot them both in the stomach, Brookshire twice, Pine five times. They died slow and hard, tangled together at the bottom of the stairs, jerking and moaning, bleeding to death.

After he'd reloaded the rifle and put it back in the house, just inside the sliding doors, he went down the stairs, turned the two men on their backs, and emptied their pockets. He took their money, their passports, airline tickets, traveller's cheques, all the papers they were carrying, and brought everything back upstairs to his bedroom. And he took Brookshire's glasses.

He went outside again then, loaded the bodies into the

back seat of their car, drove it two miles down the coast to the sea cliffs, released the brake, and rolled it over. It hit the water with a hollow smacking sound, sucked under, and stayed under.

He walked home by another road. When he got there, he turned on the outside tap and hosed down the steps and the driveway. The water ran red, then pink, then clear at last as it spread across the warm pavement and guttered off into the flower beds on the low side. Rolling the hose up carefully, he laid the coil in the dark alcove under the stairs.

Upstairs in his bedroom he studied the two passports, laid Pine's aside and concentrated on Brookshire's. Martin Brookshire: age – 37; height – five feet nine; weight – one hundred fifty-seven; hair – black; eyes – blue. Close enough. Also Brookshire was carrying most of the money – traveller's cheques, three thousand two hundred dollars in his name, and an American Express card.

Tucker took two sheets of carbon paper out of a desk drawer. In the bathroom he soaked the paper till the warm water in the sink turned ink–black. Then he stripped down, bent over the sink, and soaked his head. When he dried his hair it was several shades darker than before. When he combed it back with oil, it was darker still. Putting on Brookshire's glasses, he studied himself in the mirror, compared his face with the photo in the passport, and was satisfied. A long chance perhaps but better than no chance.

For two hours he sat at the desk and copied Brookshire's signature from the passport and the traveller's cheques. Then he put the originals away and made two pages of signatures from memory. Late in the afternoon he packed the brown leather valise they'd given him, putting in the clothes they'd bought him in Chicago. The best suit, dark brown, he left out to wear, also a new shirt and a brown and blue striped tie.

When it was nearly dark, when the quick afternoon rain had come and gone, he went into the kitchen and made four sandwiches. He ate one, washed it down with a

10

bottle of Costa Rican beer, and packed the other three in the bag with his shirts.

At full dark, when he was ready to leave, he brought a five-gallon can of gasoline up from the garage and emptied most of it on the floor, equal parts sloshed into each room. Then he soaked a ball of twine in what was left of the gas, anchored it under a chair, and backed slowly out through the rear door of the house, holding one end of the twine, playing it out till he was two hundred feet up the slope towards the back road. He secured the end of the twine with a rock, then went back to the house to wash his hands and pick up his bag.

He turned on all the lights in all the rooms and just before he left he stood in the bedroom for a long moment. Thelma's robe and nightgown were still lying across the chair, her hairbrush and powder and lipstick on the dressing table, her scent and her presence still very much there in the room.

Outside the house, on the terraced lawn where he'd buried her – the house lights barely bringing out the name THELMA TUCKER on the cross he'd made and driven into the ground – he stood at the foot of the grave, the valise on the earth beside him. He stood there for a long, silent time.

Climbing the hill behind the house again, he found the end of the twine–fuse, lighted it with a match, and watched it sputter and spit and burn slowly along its length towards the gasoline–soaked house.

On up to the crown of the slope then, to the rough back road heading northeast through a tangle of palms and vines and undergrowth, he'd walked perhaps a quarter of a mile when he sensed the sudden light–flare behind him. He looked back and saw the sky flaming yellow–orange as the house burned, shot sparks up into the blackness, and exploded at last, red and blue–white like a firebomb, when the heat and flames hit the liquid fuel tank on the back wall of the building.

CHAPTER TWO

HE WALKED ALL night, birds crying around him, night animals skittering across the road, and insects coming and going in nervous clouds. When he angled across to the main highway at last, as the sun edged up over the mountains, he was twenty miles south and east of Puntarenas. A produce truck picked him up there and took him all the way to San José.

There was a noon flight from San José to Caracas with an ongoing connection to Rio de Janeiro. Roy applied Brookshire's return ticket to Miami against the Rio fare and paid the difference with Brookshire's American Express card. He used Brookshire's District of Colombia driver's licence and his passport for identification.

The girl at the airline counter studied the passport picture carefully. 'Not a good picture of you, Mr Brookshire,' she said. But the overweight young man in passport control only glanced at the picture before he exit-stamped the passport on an empty page and waved Tucker through.

In the magazine rack on the plane, Tucker found a three-week-old Latin American edition of *Newsweek*. On the cover was a formal portrait of Neal Nelson Whittaker, the presidential seal behind him, and printed in red under the picture – 'EX-PRESIDENT ASSASSINATED'.

As he read the story inside, key phrases crystallised, isolated themselves, came to sharp visual life '. . . early

12

morning shooting at his home in the mountains east of Los Angeles . . . shots fired from a helicopter as former President Whittaker walked from his house to the swimming pool . . . killed instantly . . . helicopter destroyed by conspirators . . . escape car burned in Los Angeles forest . . . intense investigation . . . public furore.'

A few pages farther on in the magazine, Tucker found a picture of himself, the full–face identification photograph from the prison files.

Roy Tucker, 38, a recent escapee from the Indiana State Prison at Hobart, was shot to death Thursday while resisting arrest in Lethbridge, Alberta. Tucker, a convicted murderer, is also believed to have killed *Oscar Spiventa*, 55, his former cellmate at Hobart. Spiventa's body was found in the Lake Michigan dunes five miles from the prison the day after he and Tucker escaped.

According to Canadian police officials, Tucker's body was claimed by members of the US Secret Service, division of Executive Security, and flown back to Washington. Informed sources in the intelligence community speculate that Tucker may have been connected with the assassination of Neal Whittaker.

Investigations of Tucker's prison escape were slowed down this week when *Eldon Ditcher*, 51, the warden at Hobart, and *Russell Bowkamp*, 46, his deputy, died in a freak highway accident and explosion between Gary and East Chicago.

Tucker leaned back in the seat, closed his eyes, and made a mental listing of the victims so far: Spiventa, Arnold Schnaible, Whittaker, Marvin Tagge, Thelma, Ross Pine and Brookshire. Bowkamp and Ditcher, too. All dead. And now, for some reasons of their own, they were saying that *he* was dead. Some poor vagrant bastard had been killed and misidentified, just to stifle the questions and close the books.

Three people left now – just three besides himself – the woman, Helen Gaddis, and a man named Henemyer. . . And Tom Reser. No pattern of blame made any sense without Reser at the core of it.

CHAPTER THREE

THE DAY HE buried Thelma, when he believed that he would die next, in a few days probably, a week or so at most, Tucker sent a letter to Robert Applegate in Chicago:

I've seen the papers and the news magazines. What they're saying about me. I know you think I'm dead but I'm not. But I could be by the time you get this letter.

I'm not even sure why I'm writing to you. I don't expect you to do anything. It's too late for anybody to *do* anything. The damage has been done. But all the same I need to tell somebody what happened. And I don't have anybody else to tell.

The papers say I escaped from the prison at Hobart. I didn't. I walked out. It was a set–up. Warden Ditcher was in on it, and his deputy, a guy named Bowkamp.

Here's how it happened. A man named Tagge came to see me at the prison. Marvin Tagge. And later a younger man – Ross Pine. Tagge seemed like a decent guy. Pine was an asshole from the start.

They said they might be able to help me get out of prison so I listened. I knew they weren't handing me a rose on a plate. I knew I'd have to do something in return. But I didn't ask what. I didn't want to know. I just wanted out. I wanted to see Thelma again.

So I played the game. Once I got outside the walls, I thought I could out-manoeuvre them. You know me – plenty of guts but short on brains.

I had a cellmate named Oscar Spiventa. The day before

14

they were due to drive me out through the gates in a bakery truck, I said I wouldn't go if Spiventa didn't come along. They didn't like it but they backed down. But the next day, after the escape, when we transferred from the truck to a limo, in the dunes north of Hobart, they put half a dozen bullets in Oscar, cracked me on the head, and drove me to the Dorset Hotel in Chicago.

As soon as I came to, I knew I was in trouble. Pine was there, two guys named Brookshire and Henemyer – and a woman named Helen Gaddis. Brookshire was the one who'd iced Oscar. I was ready to tear somebody up. But they had me by the balls. They had Thelma. They let me talk to her on the phone but they wouldn't tell me where she was.

I was in Chicago for two days. They told me not to get in touch with you or Arnold Schnaible. You remember Arnold – the lawyer who defended me at the trial in Indianapolis. I tried to call you anyway. Couldn't reach you. But I reached Schnaible. Met him in Lincoln Park and talked with him for a while. And later that day somebody choked him to death in his office garage downtown.

They flew me to Costa Rica. Thelma was waiting there for me. And a house with my name on the deed. Plus two hundred thousand bucks in the bank – in my name! Santa Claus time. 'It's too good to be true,' Thelma said. She was right.

They left us alone for a while in Costa Rica – let us get used to the sweet life – then they flew us to California, put us in a hotel in Santa Monica. By then I'd met another guy . . . a retired general named Tom Reser.

I still didn't know what they wanted from me but I knew I was about to find out. When Reser finally told me, I said nothing doing. I don't know what I'd expected but it was nothing like that. I said I'd rather go back to jail. And I meant it. But all the time I was talking tough, when I was away from the hotel, they went back there and picked up Thelma. So I had my choice: Thelma alive or Thelma dead. It wasn't any choice at all and they knew it. If I didn't kill Whittaker, they'd kill my wife.

After Whittaker was dead, as soon as we'd landed the chopper, I saw how things were going to be. The pilot had taken a bullet from the ground from Whittaker's bodyguards. So they left him in the helicopter and blew it up. And later, after Tagge took Thelma and me to the airport to fly back to Costa Rica, his car exploded in the parking lot with him in it.

Then, the day before yesterday, a car ran over Thelma as she was walking down the road to the village near our house here. I know I'll be the next to go but I don't give a damn. I feel so lousy and sick about what I did and what they did to Thelma I don't give a damn about anything. But I guarantee you I'll take a couple of those bastards with me when I go.

I don't understand any of this stuff that's happened, Bob. I mean I don't know *why*. But, Jesus, whoever planned all this can't get away with it, can they? What about the laws? Somebody has to *pay*, don't they? If they don't, then nothing makes any sense.

CHAPTER FOUR

THERE WAS A plane change and a long delay in Caracas. It was nearly midnight when Tucker's Varig flight arrived at last in Rio, circling low across the black velvet harbour, the city brilliant with lights, vibrating with life and heat and music.

He went directly to the travellers' service desk inside the terminal. 'I need an inexpensive hotel, not too far from the water. And I want a place where they speak English.'

The taxi took him to a hotel called Bernardo's. The proprietor was a multilingual alcoholic, half French, half Portuguese, Bernardo Guzman. His wife's name was Shirley, pencil–thin and acerbic, carelessly bleached hair, suffering always from the heat, a native of Richmond, Virginia, and longing to return there.

'It's good to hear somebody talk English,' she said when Tucker checked in. 'I'm so sick of this Brazilian lingo I could throw up. It's *ugly*. You know what I mean? I hear the chatter in the streets before I get out of bed in the morning and it puts me in a stinking mood all day.' She handed him his room key and said, 'How long you think you'll be with us?'

'I'm not sure. A week or two maybe.'

He cashed some of Brookshire's traveller's cheques at Banco Suisse and bought himself a lightweight suit and a Panama hat. 'You need a hat here,' Shirley told him. 'The sun will burn your brains out if you're bareheaded. Also you have to protect your head from all the little brats taking a leak off the balconies.'

He strolled around the city, moving slowly, heavy with the wet heat, soaked with sweat, his legs and armpits chafed, his eyes burning, his cheeks flushed. And he went to a barber shop to have his hair dyed permanently black.

Sitting in cafés for hours, staying in the shade, listening to guttural mixtures of Portuguese and a dozen other languages and understanding nothing, he welcomed the sound, when he returned to the hotel, of Shirley Guzman's white–trash, slurring, Richmond drawl. 'You sound like *you're* from the South, too,' she said. 'Whereabouts?'

'West Virginia. But that was a long time ago.'

'I thought so. Takes one to know one.' Then, 'Whatever you do, don't get stuck down here. This place is the shits. Pardon my French. But there's no other word for it. One of these days I'm gonna get my act together and evacuate out of here so fast there won't be nothing left but a little puff of dust where I was standing.'

In the long hours of solitude and silence, Tucker tried to make plans. But nothing crystallised. In the wet heat, all straight lines bent and curved into circles. Instead of specific objectives and clear checkpoints, all he could find, all he could feel, was ugly anger, a need to break things, to twist and tear and gouge, to draw blood.

With no programme and no pattern, unable to select a starting place, he lost speed, became unsure about everything. Even his presence in Brazil, even *that* simple truth, disturbed him. He felt conspicuous, vulnerable, out of place. All the strange and foreign scents and sounds and flavours made him seem foreign to himself. For the first time in a crime–filled life he felt like a criminal. His reflection in store windows unsettled him. He read guilt in his face. Each time he passed a policeman, he expected to be singled out and arrested – not for past crimes, simply for undesirability, for not belonging, for being so flagrantly and clearly a misfit.

In the last days before Thelma died, Brazil had been, without question, a solution. They discussed it a lot. Having managed the escape from California to Costa Rica, Brazil seemed the obvious next step, the final step, they hoped, a place to disappear in, a primitive, uncharted space where two unremarkable faces could blend in and be lost, be safe; where, even if found, they could not be extradited. In Hobart the dullest illiterate inmate had known that. It was a prison–yard litany: 'One big score and you can live like a fucking king in Brazil.'

So they had decided Brazil was the solution. The two of them hiding forever in the shadows of a country they had never seen. It had made sense for him and Thelma, simply because nothing else made sense at all.

Tucker alone, however, was another matter. Self-preservation was no longer enough. He had no clear impulse now, no direction, no drive. He didn't know how to start or where to start. Every answer brought twenty new questions. Every notion cancelled itself. Detesting his ineptitude, he longed for Spiventa's shrewdness, Thelma's cool-headed instinct for what might work and what couldn't. Needing direction, aching for it, needing facts and maps and diagrams, he couldn't find them. So he sat on shady terraces in the brutal heat of Rio de Janeiro, sipping cool drinks, sweating, and waiting.

CHAPTER FIVE

TUCKER HAD BEEN in Brazil for nearly two weeks when he saw Helen Gaddis. On a crowded afternoon street, in the busiest downtown part of the city, she came walking towards him in a soft flowered dress, her hair grayer than he remembered, her eyes hard and straight ahead as she moved quickly through the crowds.

She was a familiar type in Rio, a well-kept lady from the North, from Boston perhaps, or Denver, a woman who had been to Europe a dozen times, to the Orient and South Africa and New Zealand, and who was curious now to discover if there was anything at all worth seeing or buying in South America. There she was, blending with the crowd in a way she had learned, moving freely, making eye contact with no one, vanishing as quickly as she had appeared.

By the time Tucker realised what he had seen, *whom* he had seen, she was gone. He turned and hurried back through the street, slicing through the crowd, straining to see ahead. He walked for two miles along the wide mosaic sidewalks taking in, *trying* to take in, every face. But he couldn't find her.

Suddenly then he became wary. Since he had seen her, she might have seen him. She, or someone, could be watching him now, from a roof top or a high window, rifle ready, cross-hairs centred cleanly on his back.

He turned off the boulevard, moved through narrow

19

angling streets, outdoor markets, and crowded stores. At last he stopped for an iced coffee in a café he had never visited before.

He sat there for an hour isolating, clear as snapshots, the times he'd seen Helen Gaddis before. First in the Dorset Hotel in Chicago where they'd brought him after the staged prison break, drugged and scared, a fresh memory in his head of Spiventa falling dead in the Dunes, Brookshire pumping bullets into him.

The second time was at the house in Santa Monica, after they'd kidnapped Thelma, then beat Tucker unconscious, and told him it was going to be *their* way or no way.

The last time he'd seen Gaddis, a few hours later, at the Santa Monica house again, she'd brought Thelma back, exchanging the pawn, releasing the hostage, the deed done now, Whittaker dead in his swimming pool, and the plane waiting to fly them, Tucker and Thelma, to Costa Rica, clear skies and smooth sailing, money in the bank, the chapter ended, the book closed.

Tucker had almost believed it. He'd needed to believe it. But after Tagge's car blew up at the airport, after he saw Thelma broken and crushed on that downhill road to the village, he'd stopped believing. After that he didn't believe in anything except ugliness and death. Only things he'd learned as a child retained their meaning: simple things he'd heard in the country church twelve miles southeast of Elkins in West Virginia – an eye is proper payment for a sacrificed eye; a tooth for a tooth.

When the waiter brought a cheque for the coffee, he handed Tucker a slip of blue paper folded twice. 'A lady left this for you,' he said.

'It can't be. I don't know anybody here.'

'A grey–haired lady. An American.'

Tucker paid the cheque, got on a crowded bus in front of the café, and rode it for nearly a mile. When he got off he walked to a bench in a grove of date palms just beside a crumbling pink building, sat down and read the note.

> They know you're here but they don't know *where*. I'm the only one who knows that. Perhaps I can help you if you use your head. And maybe you can help me. Meet me in the bar of the Hotel Queen Anna Maria at six o'clock.

Tucker tore up the note and dropped it into a trash container. Walking down the street then till he came to a theatre that showed English-language motion pictures with Portuguese subtitles, he went inside and found a seat in the last row. The first feature began at four forty–five, the second at six–thirty. When he got back to his hotel it was twenty minutes past nine.

Bernardo was behind the desk, drinking coffee and listening to symphonic music – Brahms – the volume turned low, a decanter of rum within easy reach, a black cigar balanced delicately between his first and second fingers.

'Anyone looking for me?' Tucker said.

'No one.'

'No telephone calls?'

'Nothing. Silence. A peaceful night, *grâce à Dieu*.'

Tucker climbed the stairs to his room on the fourth floor. When he unlocked the door and opened it, the phone was ringing. It was Helen Gaddis.

'You're acting like a fool. I can help you if you'll let me. Go to the pay telephone booth on the lobby floor. I'll call you there.'

In Tucker's mind she was the enemy – no question about that. The evidence was clear, the memories still fresh. He could kill her or he could run away so she couldn't kill him. Those were the choices.

His mind ping–ponged back and forth, searched for solid ground and found none. Then a new question came to him. Was Helen Gaddis perhaps capable of the truth? And in his hopeless situation wasn't a chance in one million better than no chance at all? Finding no clear answers, reaching no decisions, he went downstairs to the lobby.

Guzman had come out from behind the desk and was standing half in and half out of the public telephone booth. When he saw Tucker come down the last flight of stairs, he held out the receiver and said, 'It's for you, Mr Brookshire.'

Once he was inside the booth with the door closed, as soon as Tucker put the receiver to his ear, Helen Gaddis said, 'I don't have much time so listen carefully. I'm running too. They're after me now.'

'Don't hand me that. Why should I believe that?'

'Because you don't have any choice. You saw what happened to Tagge in California. And to your wife. They won't stop now till everybody's accounted for. You especially. Also . . . if *I* wanted to kill you, you'd be dead by now. Remember that. I'm giving you a chance to save yourself. But it's the last chance. Tomorrow morning I'll be at the Hotel Cascadura in Niteroi.'

'Where's that?'

'Across the bay. The hotel's a five-minute walk from the bridge. Don't ask for me at the desk. Come straight up. Room 537. Ten o'clock sharp. I'll see you in the morning.'

Tucker hung up slowly and said, 'Like hell you will.'

CHAPTER SIX

HE SLEPT BADLY. Lying awake, looking up at the ceiling, odd and ill-matched pieces from the past, like scraps of shredded paper, clustered and swirled in his head. Faces

22

and voices, houses and cars and grey furnished rooms in crumbling buildings, corridors and mess halls, and the piss–acrid toilets of a dozen jails and work–farms, reformatories, and prisons.

It seemed a century behind him, but close counting made it two months, a little over, only that long since that first day with Marvin Tagge, closeted in the conference room in the prison's administration building. Countless lifetimes lived since then, countless deaths. Heavy funerals in the heart – till Thelma's dying squeezed out all the blood and tears and hope that were left.

Day to day since then – going through the motions, waiting for some impulse or insight or outside action to steer him and set him in motion.

He tried to imagine what Thelma would tell him if she were here. What would she say? 'Let it *be*, Roy. You can stay alive now if you want to. Nothing's more important than *that*.' Would she say that? Something very like that surely. And Spiventa? How about him? 'Quit while you're ahead, asshole. You're out-manned and out-gunned. And besides that, they're smarter than you are. A lot smarter.'

Whatever ability Tucker had to measure his experience, to use logic and common sense, it told him as he lay there in the dark, soft night music drifting down from the *favela* on the hill behind the hotel, that *least* was *truly* best now, that nothing he could do would in any way change what had already been done. Nothing could bring back the bullets he'd fired that early October morning from the helicopter. And nothing, God knows, could bring back Thelma. Countless times during the night he came to the same conclusion. It calmed him, allowed him to cool down, grow heavy in the bed, and go to sleep.

But his dreams were ugly: bondage and torture, threats and pressures, lies and betrayal – with Thelma the hostage always. Continuing threats against her, *using* her, keeping her from him, keeping her alive, letting her live till she'd served her purpose, then killing her, suddenly and senselessly. That last sight of her flashed and re–flashed in his mind, her body crumpled soft against the base of the roadside wall, her head twisted at an ugly angle like a broken doll, her skull crushed.

Also in his dreams, illogically, outside the pattern of his conscious thoughts, the memory of his last meeting with his sister, with Enid, something he thought he had long since put behind him; the scene kept flipping back, in word–for–word clarity, across the time, seven years more or less, since he'd seen her.

It was before he'd met Thelma. Just back from Vietnam, he'd written Enid in Toronto, told her he wanted to see her. When she wrote back in her awkward handwriting, she told him she didn't think the visit was a good idea. But he went anyway.

They had sat in the kitchen for more than an hour, in her upstairs apartment in a poor frame-building neighbourhood crowded with small factories. While Tucker drank coffee, Enid struggled to manage her five–month–old baby and two–year–old twins, and attempted to explain what she hadn't made clear in her letter.

'It's Kirby that says it, Roy. It ain't *me*. But I'm his wife and I can't go against him. I told him over and over you're my only brother, the only kin I've got left practically, since Mom died and Dad went off the way he did. But Kirby just gets all red in the face and says him and these kids are what I should be thinking about now.'

She leaned over and picked the baby up off the floor. 'He says we got a chance to make something of ourselves up here in Canada where nobody cares about what poor sticks we all was down in West Virginia. Kirby's working like a dog at two jobs and making some decent wages, you got to hand it to him, and with any luck maybe we'll be able to get us a little place of our own in a year or so. Put some money down, whatever we can scratch together, and pay the rest off like rent.

'You see what I'm getting at, don't you, Roy? It's like we can start clean. Nobody up here knows about Kirby running off from the draft the way he did, nobody knows anything about where we came from, and nobody knows about . . . I mean nobody knows I've even *got* a brother.'

'What's so great about that?' Tucker said.

'Nothing. I didn't say I liked it to be like that. I *hate* it. You know how close we was as kids, you and me. But Kirby says there's no other way. He says you've been in jail most of your life and that's all you know. All you'll ever know. He says he doesn't want his kids to grow up knowing their uncle's a jailbird. *I* didn't say that. Kirby did.'

She poured more coffee in Tucker's cup. 'Besides,' she said then, 'I think he feels funny because you went in the Army and he didn't. But he won't admit that. He just says . . . like I told you. I mean he just doesn't want you around here, Roy. He was mad as hell when I got your letter saying you wanted to come and visit. I'm scared to death of what he'll say if he finds out you was here this morning.'

Other dialogues raced through Tucker's head as he lay there awake in the dark, cluttered his dreams when he fell asleep, fitfully, for a few minutes. Old half–forgotten moments with his father, with schoolteachers, with his mother and sister, long lectures from Dr Applegate in Vietnam and later in Japan, and still later in Chicago, before Thelma, long before Tagge and Pine and Brookshire and Reser, each conversation different in detail and manner but the message and the intent always clearly the same.

'You've got to get hold of yourself, Roy. You're your own worst enemy. Just use your head and *plan* a little bit and you won't keep getting into trouble.'

Like a child who says, 'I'm a bad boy,' Tucker had formed the habit, very early, of taking the blame, of looking always for the flaw in himself, and finding it quickly. Or inventing it when it couldn't be found. Each time he stood before a judge for sentencing he felt, even on the occasions when he was innocent, that he deserved whatever punishment was given him. He always went to prison willingly, accepted it, welcomed it in a way, came to feel at last that it was his proper home, the place where he belonged. Then Tagge and Pine had turned him around, offered a miracle, an alternative life, offered him Thelma again, helped him to believe in himself and some future, served up the feast and the wine, then spilled it in his lap.

All this buzzed and bubbled in Tucker's head as he rolled and turned and perspired through the night. Questions and quandaries, old guilts and scars and pains, slivers of stone and shrapnel and pieces of wire all wove themselves together somehow into a torture blanket and held him down on the mattress, wrestling and struggling.

At five in the morning he got up, stood naked in front of the window and watched the sun begin to burn red across the bay. He took a shower then, shaved, put on clean clothes, and went down to the lobby .

Shirley Guzman was sitting at a table in the tiny dining room wearing a robe, smoking a cigarette, and drinking coffee.

'You're up early,' he said.

'Always. Who can sleep in this heat? And the drums thumping back up there on the hill. They dance all night, I guess. Dance and screw and beat those lousy drums. Bernardo says they're trying to drive everybody out of Rio so they can turn it into one big *favela*. An outdoor toilet with a tin roof and samba music morning till night. And laundry hanging on long strings from every shanty.'

Tucker sat listening to her, drinking strong coffee, black and thick. His body felt sore and punished from the night. His eyes burned and his brain responded slowly. He listened to Shirley's recital of the ailments of Brazil, only half–hearing, stirring sugar into his coffee and watching her lips form the poisonous words in the half–lit, stuffy dining room of the hotel.

Forgetting his own problems then, he listened at last, when the caffeine had jolted him awake, like a man in a mezzanine seat, watching the performance unfold, curious and interested, eager to get his money's worth.

Only when he spoke finally, when he began to question her, only then did he realise that sometime in the night, some reasonable part of him had made up its mind, had cut through the emotional brambles and come to a clean decision. He had decided what he wanted. He wanted to survive.

'I want to go to some other part of Brazil.'

'Forget it. It's all crap. Take my advice and go back to wherever you came from. There's nothing to see down here. Nothing to do. If you don't want to get drunk or sniff ether, if you don't want to strip off and roll around on the beach with some fat sow, there's nothing in Rio.'

'I'm thinking of a smaller place. Just a town maybe. Someplace in the interior. Out of the way.'

'It's all out of the way. This whole crummy country is out of the way. Believe me, there's nothing to see. It's all jungle and bugs and stink. No place for a vacation.'

'I don't mean a vacation. I want to stay here for a while.'

'You're kidding.'

'I might even stay for good,' he said.

'You're crazy. You'd be dead in a year.'

'You're not dead. How long have you lived here?'

'Twelve years. Since I was twenty-two. And I've been dead since I was twenty-three. I'm walking and talking but I'm dead. *Believe* me.'

'I read in a travel folder about Petropolis. It sounds like a nice place. Up in the mountains.'

'It's a graveyard,' she said. '*Boring*. People swat flies all day and feed them to the pigeons. When the sun goes down they go to bed. And the next day they swat more flies and feed them to some more pigeons.'

Tucker said he was looking for a cooler place where he could live inexpensively. 'And I'll have to earn some money. I'm not rich. I'll have to work.'

'You want to *work*? Here in Brazil?'

'I'll have to.'

'What can you do?'

'I thought maybe I could work in a little hotel. Something like this one. Someplace where they need a man who can speak English.'

'You know how much a job like that would pay you?'

'I don't care. If I had a room and my meals that would satisfy me.'

27

She poured more coffee into his cup and listed again the hateful flaws of Petropolis. Then she said, 'We have a friend there, a French woman who runs a *pension*. I'll call her up if you want me to and see what she says. You might even go for her as a matter of fact. She's not a beauty exactly but she makes the best of what she's got.'

'That doesn't matter to me. I'm not looking for a girlfriend.'

'You don't have to be. If you work for Odette, she'll come looking for you. Middle of the night probably.'

Tucker went out into the street then and walked south toward the bay, the sun up now to his left, just crowning Sugar Loaf, beginning already to glare off the black-and-white pattern of the sidewalks.

At Avenida Delfim Moreira, he turned left and walked toward Ipanema, all the way along the wide white beach, past Praça General Osorio and into the Avenida Atlantica. He sat down there on a bench and looked out across the sand – nearly naked girls, slim and shining, all shades of black and brown, arriving already for a long day in the sun, spreading their bright beach towels, carefully arranging their bottles and scarves and clogs and thong sandals; and the black-eyed Carioca boys and young men, *moleque* and *melandro*, kicking soccer balls and wrestling with each other where the girls could see them; and mothers with small children, staking out temporary homesteads on the hot sand at the back edge of the beach.

Whatever twisted trails and side roads Tucker had wandered along during the night, whatever questions and answers, problems and solutions he had struggled with, he had never, not once, reconsidered his response to Helen Gaddis, never imagined that going across the bridge to Niteroi could bring anything but chaos – or a bullet in his forehead.

All his instincts told him he had made the wise choice, the only choice. He would go to Petropolis tomorrow, lose himself there, and become, little by little, a new person, learning the language, making his way, causing Roy Tucker, whatever he had been or failed to be, to disappear.

28

Mulling it over, tasting and testing it, he looked for flaws and found none. Not believing in luck, despising, in fact, the whole idea of luck, he began, nonetheless, to feel lucky. He had managed to turn things around, to extricate himself.

There was only one flaw, one jagged edge. Sitting there calmly by himself, feeling secure and safe, all his problems solved, it came to him slowly that everything he was planning had in fact been planned for him. Exile. Disappearance. A symbolic death. They would kill him if he forced them to, no question about that, but they would be just as well served if he simply rolled over and played dead. In Petropolis? Why not? Since a man they identified as Roy Tucker had already died in Canada, why risk killing the real one, even in Brazil, especially if he was willing to tuck his tail between his legs and vanish in some out–of–the–way *pension* in the mountains?

If Tucker's decision to be sensible, to survive, had come to him slowly and painfully, the reversal of that decision came sharp and final in a tiny sliver of a second. As he sat there on the bench, hat tilted low over his eyes, arms draped easily along the back rest, his legs stretched out in front of him, he made, just after eight o'clock that morning, a life–altering turn-about.

Feeling his strength suddenly, rejoicing in it, he decided that from that moment he would never be a captive again, never be a prisoner, never be held hostage – not even by himself.

CHAPTER SEVEN

AT EIGHT-THIRTY that morning, as Tucker stepped aboard the North Zone São Bento bus that would take him to the Niteroi bridge, Gerald Henemyer, already in Niteroi, got out of a rented Mercedes in front of the Hotel Cascadura. He walked inside, crossed the lobby to the elevators, and went up to the fifth floor. At the end of the corridor he found room 537 and knocked lightly on the door. Helen Gaddis, when she opened it, was wearing a robe over her pyjamas. 'You're early,' she said.

'I know. I've been up since four. I had a lot to do. And I thought I should get here early just in case.' He was husky and tall, short blonde hair and grey eyes, very young, no lines or trace of failure on his face.

'I told him to come at ten,' she said.

'Do you think he'll show up?'

'I think so. But we're covered either way.'

Henemyer glanced across the room. 'Can I use your bathroom?'

'Faîtes comme chez vous.'

She stood at the dresser, looked in the mirror, and brushed her hair. The toilet flushed in the bathroom, she heard water running in the sink, then it shut off and Henemyer came into the room again, wiping his hands on a small linen towel.

'How about some coffee?' she said. 'I had a pot sent up just before you got here.'

'Don't tell me we've got waffles and sausage and a couple of eggs over easy?'

'Afraid not. Just coffee.'

They sat down at a small table by the window and she filled their cups.

'How is it?' she said.

'Pretty decent coffee.'

'It better be. We're in Brazil.'

He tasted it again. 'Damn good as a matter of fact.' When he set his cup down he said, 'How do you read Tucker?'

'He sounds scared.'

'I don't know. He's a hard-nosed number.'

'But not too brilliant. And he knows it. He wasn't expecting to see us down here. He thought he was home free.'

'If he's spooked up what makes you think he'll show?'

'I just think he will,' she said. 'I can't guarantee it but I've got a hunch he'll be right on schedule.'

'I think you're wrong. I think he'll keep running.'

She shook her head. 'Too bull-headed. I think he'd rather fight than run. He'll show up.'

'Then what?'

'If he's got a gun I think he'll use it. At least he'll try to use it.'

'We can handle that.'

'I know we can if we have to. But I think the other wrinkle is better. Reser's right about that.'

'Everything's right if it works. If it doesn't work, it's cold chicken soup.'

'I don't know why you're worried. What can he do?' she said.

'You tell me. He's got information and he's got a mouth. That combination scares the hell out of me.'

'Who would he tell? Who would believe him?'

'Nobody maybe. But I'd hate to see his face on the seven o'clock news.'

'Never happen. And you know it.'

'Three weeks ago we never thought he'd get out of Costa Rica.'

31

'Pine got careless.'

'That's right. And that's what I don't want to do. I am very anxious not to get careless.'

She stood up then and said, 'I'd better pull myself together. I'm not accustomed to gentleman callers before I've brushed my teeth.'

Inside the bathroom, she closed the door behind her and snapped the lock. She stood with her ear pressed against the door. After a moment she heard Henemyer's cup click on his saucer and the different sound of his spoon stirring, then coming to rest on the saucer.

She moved quickly away from the door and took a soft, tissue–wrapped package out of her make–up case. Before she folded it open, she flushed the toilet and turned on both taps in the sink. She took a snub–nose .32 calibre revolver out of the tissue paper, unwrapped a silencer, locked it on the muzzle, and slipped the gun into the pocket of her robe. She listened at the door again till she heard the click of Henemyer's coffee cup, then she turned back to the sink, creamed her face lightly, and rinsed it off with warm water.

Taking her toothbrush out of a clear plastic tube, she squeezed a ribbon of toothpaste on the bristles and carefully brushed her teeth. She uncapped her mouthwash bottle then, tipped it up, half–filled her mouth, and began to gargle. She coughed and choked suddenly, breathed the liquid into her nose, and swallowed half of it before she could spit it out. Instantly her insides from her tongue to her stomach began to burn and contract. Already dying, she jerked the revolver out of her bathrobe pocket, wrenched open the bathroom door, and trying to aim the gun at Henemyer, squeezed off one soft, muffled shot into the floor before the cyanide burned into her brain and she slumped dead on the carpet, her lips frothing pink and the skin around her mouth turning black.

CHAPTER EIGHT

As THE CITY bus came near the east end of the Rio Niteroi bridge, Tucker could see the electric sign on the roof of the Hotel Cascadura, a quarter of a mile south, on the shore looking west towards Rio.

He got off at the first stop past the end of the bridge and walked along the river–edge street toward the hotel.

It was five minutes before ten when he went up in the elevator and found room 537. The door was partly open. When he knocked, Henemyer said, 'Come in.' He stood up as Tucker came through the door and crossed to meet him, Helen Gaddis' revolver held loosely in his hand. He closed the door and snapped the lock. 'I hate to play policeman with you but I have to give you the once–over. You know the drill.'

Tucker stood with his hands on top of his head as Henemyer frisked him. Henemyer walked back to a chair then and sat down, put the revolver on the table in front of him, and indicated that Tucker should sit on the couch.

When Tucker sat down Henemyer said, 'Helen Gaddis is dead. She took poison about an hour ago. If you don't believe me you can look for yourself.' He nodded his head in the direction of the bathroom.

'I believe you.'

'She was scared stiff about something. I thought maybe I could help her but she didn't give me much of a chance. Went in the bathroom to brush her teeth and next thing I know she's dead. I feel like hell about it.'

'I'll bet you do.'

'She was a terrific woman. Tough and smart. And all of a sudden she turned to oatmeal. Makes me feel lousy.' He lit a cigarette, leaned back in his chair and said, 'What did she promise you?'

'Nothing. She called and said she wanted to talk to me. Said maybe she could help me.'

'How do you mean?'

'I don't know. She didn't say. I figured I had nothing to lose so I came to see her.'

'Yeah . . . well . . .' Henemyer made a little gesture with his hand – futility, end of the line – then, 'So you made it to Brazil?'

'That's right.'

'How do you like it?'

'I don't.'

'So what's your next move?'

'That depends on you,' Tucker said.

'How do you mean?'

'I mean you're sitting there with a pop–gun in front of you and I'm clean. So you get to make the rules.'

'No, I don't,' Henemyer said. He picked up the revolver and slid it into his jacket pocket. 'Things have changed. We don't have any hold on you now. Gaddis didn't have any orders to contact you. She did that on her own. Like I said, she was jumping at shadows. As far as we're concerned you're free as a bird. You can do whatever you want to.'

'Bullshit. Do I look like I just hatched out of an egg?'

'No, you don't. That's why I'm telling you the truth. We made a deal with you. I mean Tagge and Pine did. And Tom Reser. You kept your part of the bargain and we kept ours . . .'

'Like hell you did. Somebody killed my wife and I was next in line. Pine and Brookshire would have buried me if I . . .'

'Wrong, Tucker. You got it all wrong. We had no reason to kill your wife. We had nothing to do with that. The way I understand it, it was an accident. A car ran her down . . .'

'That's right. And that woman in there in the bathroom killed herself. And Tagge blew himself up in his car at the Burbank Airport . . .'

'Wait a minute. Tagge was something else altogether. That was politics. He came down on the wrong side, I guess. I don't know the answer to that one. But one thing I can guarantee you. Nobody gave any instructions to kill you *or* your wife.'

'And nobody withdrew my money from the bank at Puntarenas.'

'You got me there. That was a horse on us. On Pine. He was the one who pulled your money out of that bank. Reser blew his stack when he heard about it. That's why Pine and Brookshire were coming to see you that last time, to tell you the money had been put back, all two hundred thousand of it, in your name. It's still there, Tucker. It's *your* money. All you have to do is whistle and we can transfer it to a bank here in Brazil.'

'Too late. I don't want your fucking money.'

'You will. You'll change your mind. And it will be there. I promise you. As far as we're concerned, our original deal with you still holds. You stay out of the country for five years, till the whole Whittaker thing is ancient history, then you can go where you want to and do whatever you want to do.'

When they left the hotel, they drove back across the bridge to Rio, Tucker at the wheel, Henemyer beside him, Helen Gaddis' luggage packed in the trunk.

Henemyer was relaxed and friendly, his hand close to the jacket pocket holding the revolver, but no menace in his words or his manner.

'I know you thought we were a bunch of computerised bastards. And I admit it must have looked that way. But we were under the gun, we had a bitch of a job to do and there wasn't any time to be polite. Once we'd picked you and eased you out of jail, we had to stay on the rails. No time to change signals. So when you started to play rough we had to play rough too. The problem was that most of us didn't know what the game was, we didn't know what was going on, and the ones who did know couldn't tell. Pine knew what was up. And Tagge. And Reser. But the rest of us were as much in the dark as you were. When I found out we were targeted on Whittaker I couldn't believe it. To me he was just a sweet dumb guy who got elected president because he was a war hero.

'But now it's starting to come out. That sweet old man was a con artist. He'd had a kickback deal going with South Vietnam all during that shit over there. Every time we sent them ten million dollars for defence, *one* million of it went into a Zurich account, a numbered account, and only Whittaker knew the number. *Ten per cent.* That's what he got. Just like an agent's commission. He had so much money over there he couldn't even count it, let alone spend it. So you see what I'm talking about? It wasn't the way it looked to you. We weren't getting rid of a nice old white–haired man. We were handling a dangerous security risk.'

'What security? How do you figure that? We've been out of Vietnam for a long time now.'

'That's right. That's not the problem. The problem is that the South Vietnamese kept financial records. At least they kept them till somebody grabbed them and carried them up to Hanoi. And from there they got to Peking. You get the picture? All of a sudden the top men in China knew something smelly about Papa Whittaker, something he didn't want anybody else to know.

'So they started to lean on him for information. And he had a lot of it. Not only what had gone on during his administration but what's going on now. As an ex–president he could get any information he wanted – from the National Security Council, from the Pentagon, from anyplace. He was feeding microfilm to Peking by the bushel. And it couldn't be stopped because nobody knew what he was doing. Except two or three men. And they couldn't blow the whistle because it could have meant war with China. Or at the very least a break in relations at a bad time. So they stopped Whittaker the only way they could.'

'Why you telling me all this stuff?'

'Because I'm a nice guy. And because it doesn't matter now. We got the job done. *That's* all that matters. Mostly *you* got the job done. The strange fact is that if everybody knew the truth you'd be some kind of a hero. But – that's the way it goes. The history books hardly every get it right.'

When they pulled up in front of Tucker's hotel, Henemyer said, 'We'll be in touch with you. I'll make a call today and have your money transferred here to Rio. You went through a lot for us and we want to make sure you're taken care of. The other thing, about your wife – I know how you feel. I'm married with three kids myself. But I swear to God that nobody, none of us, had anything to do with her being killed.'

'I don't believe that.'

'I know you don't. But it's the truth.'

Tucker got out of the car, crossed the sidewalk, and went into his hotel. He walked up the four flights to his room, his head pounding with conflicting facts, trying to separate the truth from the lies, believing nothing one instant and everything the next.

Outside in the street, Henemyer walked to a public phone booth, dropped in a coin, and signalled for the operator. When she answered he said, in Portuguese, 'Emergency. Give me the police.' Waiting calmly then, he watched the traffic on the street behind him. When the connection was made he said, 'A woman has been killed. Hotel Bernardo in the Leblon section. She is in room 44.'

Upstairs, Tucker walked down the fourth-floor corridor to his room, unlocked the door, and went inside. The window shades were drawn and all the lights were on. Shirley Guzman was lying naked on top of the bed, Tucker's pyjama jacket half on her shoulders, his blue–and–brown necktie knotted tight around her throat. Her face had begun to turn dark, her tongue, black and swollen, filled her mouth, and her eyes, bulging open, stared whitely at the ceiling light. Thrown across her lower legs were Tucker's pyjama pants, stiff with semen and dried blood.

Standing there, cold and immobile, Tucker heard the

honking wail of a Rio police car. Moving to the window, he spread the drapes and looked down at the street. Henemyer's car was still at the curb. As the police car pulled up in front of the hotel and the officers spilled out, Henemyer stood watching them, leaning against his car and smoking a cigarette, as they ran across the wide sidewalk and into the hotel.

It flashed clear then to Tucker – chilling truth, an icicle in the heart. He wheeled away from the window and began to run. Into the hallway, up two flights of stairs, down the corridor to the back of the hotel, out through the window, and down the fire escape to the alley. Keeping to the alleys for three blocks, he came out on a busy street at last and boarded the first passing bus. He rode it for half a mile, then stepped off and got into a taxi waiting at the curb. 'Aeropuerto,' he said. 'International Airport.'

CHAPTER NINE

THE FOLLOWING EVENING Henemyer sat in a restaurant in Washington D.C., with Thomas Reser, a slim, chiselled man with iron–grey hair, a neat moustache, and the delicate hands of a pianist.

'I don't know how he managed it,' Reser said.

'Neither do I. Everything was timed perfectly. But he just wasn't there. Disappeared.' Henemyer snapped his fingers. 'Whoever drove him to the airport must have set a speed record because by the time I got there he was already gone. Took the first flight out.'

'Barbados, you said.'

'That's right.'

'Now what?'

'I think he'll vamp for a few days, then come on north. Miami maybe. New York. Somewhere. We're plugged into all the airlines. We'll know when he's flying.'

'He's still using Brookshire's papers?'

'He has to. He doesn't have any of his own. No money either. If we cut off Brookshire's credit cards and traveller's cheques, Tucker won't have a dime.'

Reser poured half a pony of brandy into his coffee and tasted it. 'I don't think so,' he said. 'Let's not do that. Whatever he has in mind I'd like him to think he's making progress. I don't want him to panic.' He sipped some more coffee. 'I don't think he's a problem but he's a goddamned nuisance. This business should have been all tied up by now. Gaddis should have been our last move. But instead we've got Tucker on the loose, buzzing around like a horsefly. I don't understand it. The book on him was clear and clean – habitual criminal, not too bright – but he's been a stubborn pain–in–the–ass right from the start. He outmanoeuvred Pine and Brookshire, caught them with their pants down. How he did that I'll never know. And now, after all the trouble we went to in Brazil, he wiggled out of that. We should have given some hophead fifty dollars to cut his throat and let it go at that.'

Henemyer shook his head. 'Our other idea was better. He'd have been buried in jail down there for the rest of his life.'

'It may have been a good idea but it didn't work. We're still stuck with him. And the timing is lousy.'

'If you're really worried, let's nail him in Barbados.'

'I don't think so,' Reser said. 'If they find a body and start an investigation down there we can't control it. All we need is for somebody to identify him as Roy Tucker and people will start wondering who that other Roy Tucker was, the one the police shot up in Canada. The Whittaker thing is starting to calm down but one new piece of information and it could flare up again.'

'It won't happen, Tom. Believe me. It's painted over now. There's nobody but you and me . . .'

'And Tucker. He's still with us. And don't forget about Applegate.'

'Applegate's got a family to think about. We don't have to worry about him.'

'We didn't have to worry about Tucker either. At least that's what we thought. But the son–of–a–bitch is still around. Everybody's looking at me through a magnifying glass and it makes the hair stand up on the back of my neck.'

'Is there a firm date for the Riyadh meeting?'

'There is now. We settled it this afternoon. December 20th. I make the General Assembly speech on the 18th and we fly to Saudi Arabia that night.'

'Three weeks time,' Henemyer said. 'I think you're right. For the moment the best way to handle Tucker is to contain him. We'll know where he is and what he's up to. If he wants anything we'll give it to him. We'll kiss his ass till after December 20th. Then, after the Middle East thing is locked in, we'll lose him. He'll disappear.'

'He's a crazy bastard. Nothing scares me more than a goddamned redneck.'

'Leave him to me. I can handle him. There's no way he can hurt us. I promise you.'

CHAPTER TEN

TUCKER STAYED IN Barbados for three days. On the fourth day he flew to Miami, checked into a motel near the airport and called Dr Applegate in Chicago.

He couldn't reach him at the hospital. And an answering service picked up when he called his office. Finally, at nine o'clock in the evening, he called his home in Oak Park. When Applegate answered, Tucker said, 'It's me, Bob. Roy Tucker.'

There was a long silence. Then '. . . Jesus Christ.'

'I need to see you. I have to talk to you.'

'The papers said you were dead.'

'They rigged that. I wrote you about that.'

'What?'

'Didn't you get the letter I sent from Costa Rica?'

'I don't know what you're talking about.'

'Jesus, Bob, I sent you a registered letter. The whole story about what happened.'

'I didn't get any letter.'

'But how . . .?'

'I told you. I didn't get a letter from you.'

'All right. Look, Bob, I have to see you. I'm coming to Chicago.'

'Where are you now?'

'In Miami.'

'I mean what's your number there? I can't talk on this phone. I'll go in the den and call you back on the other line.'

'I'm in a motel. 305–321–6000. Room 217.'

'I'll call you back in three minutes.'

Tucker waited by the phone for two hours. Applegate didn't call. When he dialled his house again, no one answered. He called the office number then and gave his Florida number to the message service. 'It's very important. Ask Dr Applegate to call me right away.'

'Yes, sir. I'll give him your number as soon as he checks in.'

He knew when he hung up the receiver that Applegate wouldn't call. It was painful knowledge. It made him feel hollow suddenly – cut off and weaponless.

He stayed in his room all the next day. And all that night till four in the morning. Then he checked out. The night clerk called him a taxi and he rode to the Greyhound Bus depot in downtown Miami. The first bus out was going to Jacksonville. Tucker bought a one–way ticket.

Before he got on the bus he bought a ball–point pen and a stiff–backed school pad with blue–lined paper. Sitting near the back of the coach as it wheeled out of the terminal and headed north, he began to write, carefully and laboriously, in the notebook.

My name is Roy Tucker. I was born in Underhill, West Virginia, 27 January 1943. I've been in one jail or another most of the time since I was a kid. Except when I was in Vietnam. The last time they convicted me for killing a man named Riggins. He was my wife's first husband. They sent me to Indiana State Prison at Hobart, twenty years to life.

Tucker sat back and looked out the bus window. Then he read over what he had written. Finally he started to write again.

Sometime last September, early in the month, Warden Ditcher had me brought up to his office. He introduced me to a man named Marvin Tagge. Later I met another

42

man named Ross Pine. And after that I met a guy named Tom Reser who said he used to be a general . . .

CHAPTER ELEVEN

'IF THIS GUY is dumb,' Reser said, 'I'll take vanilla. We sit here deciding what we're going to do to him and meanwhile he's figured out what he's going to do with *us*.' He was sitting behind the desk in the study of his house in Georgetown, two–thirty in the morning, Henemyer seated across from him, an opened envelope on the desk top between them, two Xerox pages and a handwritten note on blue–lined paper.

'He's scared,' Henemyer said.

'*He's* scared! *I'm* scared. I've got ambassadors and senators and bankers lined up all over Washington waiting to kiss my ass. They know we're up to something big but they don't know what. I'm King Shit in this town because I've got a secret.' He got up, walked to the liquor cart, and poured himself a drink. 'And what am I doing? I'm staying up nights trying to outmanoeuvre some third–rate jailbird who's got me by the short hair.'

'I'm telling you, Tom, he's just trying to buy some time.'

'Bullshit. You read those pages. Are you saying that's nothing to get excited about? He's got it all spelled out, chapter and verse, every move we made from the time Tagge and Pine started to slide him out of jail. Who did what, who said what, every goddamned detail of the

43

Whittaker thing. He even spelled my name right.'

'So what? What can he do with it? Nobody's gonna print that junk. You think the *Post* or the *Times* would pick up a piece of crap like that? Can you see Roger Mudd reading that on camera? They get a hundred pieces of lunatic mail like that every day.'

'That's right. I know that. The only difference is this piece of crap happens to be *true*.'

'True or false, what's the difference? If nobody prints it . . .'

'Let me tell you something. There's always somebody around who's willing to print *anything*. There's an underground paper now in every city in the country. They thrive on stuff like this. It pays the rent. And with my name on it, it's dynamite. Haven't you been reading the papers? The Israelis say I'm anti-Semitic, the pacifists say I'm a war-monger, and the Pentagon says I'm soft on Cuba. Since we started sending up trial balloons about new arms quotas nobody likes me but the Arabs.'

'What does that have to do with Tucker?'

'Everything. I'm telling you if this story of his shows up *anywhere* before I finish the job they're sending me to Saudi Arabia for, the whole fucking ballpark could blow up in our faces.' He picked up the piece of blue-lined paper and slid it across to Henemyer. 'Read this. Read what he says.'

'I read it.'

'I know you did. But read it again. Read it out loud this time and *listen* to it.'

Henemyer picked up the sheet of paper.

'Go ahead,' Reser said, 'you'll see what I mean.'

'"Here's something I just wrote out today,"' Henemyer read in a monotone. '"Everything about what happened in Chicago and California and Costa Rica. Don't get me wrong. I'm no hero. I don't give a damn if anybody finds out the truth or not. But the way I figure it there's nobody left now who knows what went on except you and me and Henemyer. All I care about is saving my own skin. If you lay off me I'll forget I ever saw you. But just in case I end

44

up in a ditch someplace with my face blown off I want you to know that a friend of mine has twenty Xerox copies of this story in stamped envelopes, sealed and addressed to people who might want to know what happened to Whittaker. I call this friend of mine every Sunday morning. If any Sunday goes by and he hasn't heard from me, he'll go down to the post office the next morning and mail off all these envelopes I left him.

'"Right now I'm at a rooming house in Savannah on Front Street. The place is called Martha Clymer's. I'll be here for a week or so. I'm still using Brookshire's name. *And* his money. But I could use some more. Roy Tucker."'

CHAPTER TWELVE

NINE O'CLOCK AT night. A cold winter rain falling in Chicago. And in Oak Park, a suburb just west of the city, in a blocky early Frank Lloyd Wright house, Corinne Applegate, thirty–five years old, tall and slender, with short–cropped honey–blonde hair, was angry and crying.

'My God, Bob, what do you expect me to say?' They were in their bedroom with the door closed, their two daughters, Liza and Brooke Ann, doing their homework in the family room downstairs. 'You're like a phantom. I mean ever since Roy Tucker broke out of jail . . .'

'That has nothing to do with anything,' Applegate said. He was tall too, over six feet, regular features, an open face, and ginger–red hair. 'I haven't seen Roy for more than five years and you know it.'

'I don't know anything.'

'I haven't seen him since his trial. Besides, he's dead now. You read the same story I did.'

'Then if it's not that, if it's not him, what is it? You jump every time the phone rings. You sit up half the night. You think I don't know why we took that sudden trip to Scotland in October? You think I didn't see through that? You didn't want to be any place where Tucker could reach you. Isn't that right?'

'No.'

'Yes, it is. I can tell by looking at you. You're a terrible liar.'

'I'm not lying, damn it.'

'Yes, you are. You know it and I know it. But I don't understand it. Roy was your friend. You were going to re–do his whole life. You practically adopted him. You brought him home from Vietnam like he was an orphan . . .'

'That's a long time ago. He was only here for a few weeks.'

'That wasn't your fault. You didn't want him to leave. He just picked up and disappeared in the middle of the night. And you acted as if your own kid had run off.'

'I was disappointed. I thought I could get him to go to school. Make something of himself.'

'He made something of himself all right. A few months after he left here he was on trial for murder.'

'Yeah . . . well . . . I don't know. What's the point, Corinne? Why are you bringing all that up now?'

'Because it's the only answer I can think of. I come into the room and find you packing a bag. What do you expect me to say?'

'I wish you'd hold your voice down a little. There's no point dragging the kids into this.'

'Why try to fool them? If they don't know tonight, I'll have to tell them tomorrow.'

'Just tell them I had to go away for a few days.'

'How many days?'

'I'm not sure. I have to work it out.'

She sat down on the edge of the bed. 'I give up, Bob. I really do. I know you wouldn't be acting like this if you didn't have a reason. I know you, for God's sake. All I can figure is that you're in some kind of trouble. But why can't you tell me what it is? Why all the mystery?'

'It's not that. I'm not trying to be mysterious.'

'Then what do you call it?'

'I don't call it anything.'

'What do I tell the hospital?' she said. 'And what about your office patients?'

'Craig can cover the office. And he and Keith will divide up the hospital stuff. I already talked to them about it.'

'So I'm the last to know. Right?'

'This is no picnic for me, honey. Don't make it worse.'

'Make it worse? Do you think I'm trying to make it worse? I'm trying to make sense out of something that scares me to death. You don't see yourself. You haven't really looked at yourself these last few weeks. I know something awful's going on in your head but why can't you tell me what it is? I'm not a cry–baby, you know. I could help you. I know I could. But first you have to open up. You have to let me in on it. You have to tell me what's happening.'

He pulled her up from the bed and put his arms around her. Finally he said, 'I can't tell you. I want to but I can't.'

47

CHAPTER THIRTEEN

IN A TELEVISION studio in Washington, DC, Archer Guernsey, senior White House correspondent for the National Broadcasting Company, sat across a table from Tom Reser, waiting for the red light on his camera to blink on. The floor manager edged in beside the camera and said, 'Film rolling . . . still rolling . . . close to the edge . . . coming up on you, Archer . . . go!' The camera light snapped on red and Guernsey began to talk.

'Our guest for this segment is Thomas Reser, military advisor to two presidents, a distinguished combat officer in three wars and a man very much in the public eye just now as architect of what seems to be a new arms policy in the Middle East. What is our position, General? Is our policy changing vis–à–vis Israel and the Arab states?'

'I don't believe change is the proper word. We think of it as an adjustment. We feel we have a responsibility to be cautious and even–handed. Balance is the key word. Stability. We would not like to see the scale tip too far in any direction.'

'Begin and his people have been quite outspoken in their criticism of what they fear will be a new US policy. And they have been especially critical of you, and of your long–time close relationships with some of the Arab leaders.'

'It's true. I do know and respect the leaders of many of the Arab states. Before I retired from active service, I

48

functioned as a senior advisor in Syria, Saudi Arabia, Egypt, and Iran. But my military judgements are in no way influenced by those old friendships and associations.'

'You have said repeatedly that you feel the best chance for peace in the Middle East is a true balance of power.'

'That's true. If each country has sophisticated military potential, if they all have jet aircraft and tanks and rockets along with the counter-weapons, if each is aware of the other's strength, there is, in my judgement, very little chance that anyone will want to start a fire–fight.'

'Senator Newgate of New Jersey said in an interview yesterday that the opposite is true. He believes that when weapons are available, people will use them.'

'Senator Newgate is not a military man.'

'He maintains that if the combined strength of the Arab states is greater than that of Israel, it's only a question of time before they use that military power to destroy Israel.'

Reser smiled and touched his moustache. 'Senator Newgate, as you know, is an old adversary of mine. I think, as I always have, that he is ill-informed and oddly motivated. It's important to remember that he, more than any other man, influenced President Truman to recall MacArthur. And he seriously weakened our efforts in Vietnam by his careless public statements, his criticism of our national policies, and his open support of young men who evaded the draft. If we listened to Senator Newgate, the Pentagon would be turned into a shopping centre.'

'In military matters you are often described as a hawk. Is that accurate? Do you think of yourself as a hawk or a dove?'

'I don't think of myself as any kind of bird. I'm a political realist. There is only one way to negotiate and that's from strength. In the world as we know it, that means *military* strength. No matter what Newgate says.'

'Can you tell us if the President has reached a final decision on the question of Arab arms?'

'Let me put it this way. I am authorised to say that the discussions are ongoing and that all decisions will be finalised before my address to the General Assembly on December 18th.'

'Can you comment on the fact that your name has been mentioned for a cabinet post?'

'I could comment but I won't. I think the best way I can serve is the way I am serving now.'

'As the President's advisor?'

'That's right.'

'One last thing, General Reser. We know that you were also an advisor to President Whittaker when he was in office.'

'That's true. I knew him for twenty years.'

'It's more than six weeks now since his assassination and the country is still in a state of shock. I realise it's a painful subject for you but do you have any thoughts about his death? What does it tell us about our country, about ourselves perhaps?'

'My grief is very personal. Neal Whittaker was the best friend I had in public life. I envied his intelligence and admired his integrity. It is incredible to me that anyone could want him dead, that any individual or any group could benefit in any way from his death.'

'I'm sure you are aware of all the conspiracy theories.'

'I am and I don't believe any of them. I am convinced that Neal Whittaker's death was an act of terrorism, a mad–dog killing by some crack–pot group – far left perhaps, some home–grown version of the Red Brigades, who knows? I was an intimate friend of J. Edgar Hoover and I stand second to no one in my admiration for the Bureau he gave us, but some old soldier instinct tells me that we'll never know the complete details of Neal Whittaker's death, who killed him or why.'

CHAPTER FOURTEEN

ON A COOL overcast afternoon in Savannah, Tucker walked down by the wharfs, strolled through the narrow streets and alleys till he found a gun shop, cashed one of Brookshire's traveller's cheques, and bought a .44 calibre automatic.

'You're not a local man, are you?' the woman behind the counter asked him.

'No, I'm not. Just here for a few days. Heading back to Chicago any time now.'

'I'll have to turn your name in. It's the law down here. Martin Brookshire . . . is that it?'

'That's right.'

'Nobody's gonna come looking for you. You don't have to worry about that. It's just a matter of record so we got something to show in case some politician gets antsy or the TV people in Atlanta start kicking up a fuss so they can sell more breakfast food. I mean, around here, if you want to have a gun, folks figure it's your own affair. Course if you want to carry it in your pocket, you're supposed to go to the police for a permit. But hardly anybody bothers themselves with that. Because nobody's apt to search you. Course in your case, if you're aiming to fly up to Chicago, you can't keep it on you. I guess you know that. Those cameras there at the security line will pick it up right away. They'll even spot it every so often in your checked suitcases. Most people I know get a couple of tin pie-pans and tape their pocket gun in between them before they pack it. Then she don't show up on the airport snooper-machine. It's little tricks like that a person learns.'

The next morning, after he ate breakfast in the downstairs dining room of Mrs Clymer's house, Tucker went back up to his room, sat in the chair by the window that looked out toward the water, and leafed through the Atlanta paper. Just before ten o'clock, Mrs Clymer came to the door and said, 'There's a fella downstairs says he wants to see you. A nice–looking man. Yellow hair. Looks like he ought to play a good game of baseball.'

'Did he tell you his name?'

'Hennigar, I think he said.'

'Henemyer.'

'Maybe. I don't know. You want to come down or should I send him on up?'

'Send him up, I guess.'

When Henemyer came through the doorway, Tucker held his hand out, palm up, the automatic resting there. 'My turn,' he said. 'Just close the door so we don't wake anybody up and put your hands on top of your head. You know the drill.'

'I'm not packing,' Henemyer said.

'I know. You wouldn't hurt a fly. Turn around.' He checked all pockets, jacket and pants, and ran one hand up and down Henemyer's sleeves and pant legs. 'Jesus, you're telling the truth,' Tucker said. 'It's enough to give me a heart attack.' He slipped the gun into his jacket pocket and they sat down, Henemyer in the chair, Tucker on the edge of the bed.

'I guess Reser got my letter. I figured if I sent it to the Pentagon, they'd send it along to him.'

'Yeah, he got it.'

'How'd he like it?'

'He thinks you're bluffing.'

'Maybe I am,' Tucker said.

'But he can't be sure.'

'That's right. He can't.'

Henemyer took a long envelope out of his inside jacket

pocket and handed it to Tucker. 'You asked for some money.'

'How much?'

'Two thousand. Tens and twenties.'

'That's a hundred and ninety-eight thousand short.'

'That was only if you stayed out of the country. That deal's off now.'

'No, it's not,' Tucker said. 'That money was promised to me, more than once, and I want it. You were right. You said I'd end up asking for the money and that's what I'm doing.'

'I don't know. I'll have to talk to Reser.'

'I don't care who you talk to. Just get it to me – a bank cheque, made out to cash. I'm leaving here in two days and I want it before I go.'

'I can't do it in two days,' Henemyer said.

'Sure you can. Work it out: if you can handle all that fancy stuff you put together down in Rio you can manage to get me a cashier's cheque.'

'What fancy stuff?'

'You know what I mean. When you dropped me off at the hotel that morning there was a dead lady in my bed. Somebody choked her to death with my necktie.' Before Henemyer could answer, Tucker held up one hand to silence him. 'Don't tell me. I already know. It's news to you. Right?'

'That's right.'

'If somebody caught you in the hen house with a dead chicken you'd swear to Christ it committed suicide.'

'Never mind the jokes. I get a salary cheque twice a month. I'm just a working man like everybody else.'

'That's what Tagge said to me once. Something like that. And five minutes later he was dead.'

'I told you before. I don't know anything about that.'

'You don't know anything about anything. I'm surprised you don't sprout wings. You're so fucking innocent you bring tears to my eyes – you and Reser. I saw him on television the other day talking about Whittaker and I thought he was gonna break down and bawl.'

53

'What did you expect him to say?'

'Just what he said, I guess. I just didn't think he'd be so good at it.'

'Reser's a very experienced guy.'

'Yeah, I guess so.'

'You asked about your letter. I'll tell you the truth. He doesn't like it but he knows you've got us over a log. So whatever you want . . .'

'I told you what I want. I want the money.'

'You'll get it. You'll have it in the morning.' Then, 'Are you planning a little trip maybe?'

'I wouldn't be surprised. But don't worry. I'll send you a postcard so you'll know where I am.'

Henemyer stood up and put on his topcoat. 'We always know where you are.'

CHAPTER FIFTEEN

WHEN TUCKER WAS fifteen years old they sent him to the juvenile work farm west of Buckhannon. Seven counts of auto theft. When he got out two years later, he hitched a ride to Bluefield to see if he could locate his father. He hadn't seen him since his mother was buried five years before in the Elkins Cemetery.

He found him finally in a second-floor room with a kitchenette in a run-down frame house on the north side of the railroad yards. He was living with a woman he called Aggie, an angular woman with dyed red hair. She wore a black rayon kimono with a red dragon on the back and her orange lipstick was smeared around her mouth.

Aggie made a fuss over Tucker. 'You're sure a lot more growed-up than your pictures. Looks to me like you'll soon be tall as your dad.' She kissed him on the mouth. Her lips were soft and pulpy and slick with the orange lipstick.

'I hope you're fixing to stay on with us a little bit. We can bed you down in the corner over there. Or maybe you can stay down the block with my sister Doris if you'd like that better. You might go for Doris. And I guarantee you she'd go for you. Mom used to say Doris liked anything in pants. But my brother, Bud, said Mom had it wrong. He said, "Doris only likes 'em when they got their pants off." He was a pistol, that kid. The shipped him off to Korea when he was only nineteen and he got his whole insides blowed out the second week he was there. Never knew what hit him, they said.'

Tucker walked with his father to a tavern down the street and they drank some beer, spending Tucker's separation money from the work farm, sitting at a wooden sawhorse table covered with oilcloth, coffee cans for ashtrays.

'What do you think of Aggie?' his father said.

'Seems like a nice enough woman.'

'Nice ain't the word for it. She saved my bacon. No two ways about it. After your mother died, and after I lost my hand the way I did, I wasn't fit for nothing. All the mill work up home had petered out and I didn't know what to do with myself. Just lay around and suck on a bottle of white mule was about all I was good for. I guess I'd have most likely soused myself right into the graveyard if it hadn't been for Aggie. I met her in some beer joint up by Weston and it was her that coaxed me to come down here to Bluefield. She said, "Like as not you can scare up some work there. But work or not, I'll look after you," And that's what she did. Good as her word. I don't know how I would have managed without her.'

'What kind of work you been doing?'

'Well, there ain't a hell of a lot of jobs for a man with a stump instead of a hand. But I was making out pretty good – light work, odds and ends. Then I fell off the top of a freight car, fifteen feet to the ground, and that was it. I ain't been fit to work a lick ever since.'

'When was that?'

'Almost three years ago now. It was Christmas week I fell. Ice all over everything and down I went.'

'So you can't work at all now?'

'Can't bend over. Can't lift anything or handle tools. I was getting disabled payments for a while but then those cheques stopped coming too. I'm entitled to it, people tell me, but the government just won't turn it loose. So, like I say, I'd be all the way up shit creek if it wasn't for Aggie.'

'What's she work at?'

'Everything. She's a working fool. You'd never guess it to look at her. Looks like she's out for a good time and to hell with everything else. But she'll fool you. She's on the go morning to night. Bakes ten or twelves pies every morning for that little eating place we passed on the way up here. She'll take in as high as five dollars a day on her pies. And she does needlework for everybody in this end of town, mending mostly for the men that live by themselves. But she can cut a pattern too. And stitch up a dress or a shirt before you hardly know she's started in. There's somebody at the door almost any time you open it looking for Aggie to do some kind of tailor work. That'll bring her maybe thirty or forty dollars a week. And as if that ain't enough, she works here in the tavern six nights a week, waiting tables or serving behind the bar or making sandwiches back in the kitchen. That brings her three dollars a night and whatever she gets in tips. And besides the money, me and her both get whatever we want to drink for no charge at all. So I'm in here every night from supper–time on.

'Sim Ealy, that owns this place, is as nice a man as you'd ever want to meet. Knows how to make a person feel welcome. Won't let you go home sober if he can help it. And like I say, it's all on the house for Aggie and me. It's like a miracle out of the Bible, Roy. I mean a man living by himself with no work and nothing coming in could go crazy as hell in no time. So I got a lot to thank Aggie for.'

'What about Enid? What do you hear from her?'

'Don't hear much. I'm no hand to write and neither is she. But she's still over there in Chilicothe with her Aunt Ethel and Uncle Howard. They sent a snapshot a year or so ago and it looks like Enid's getting to be a big grown–up girl. Favours your mother's people. You remember Aunt Hazel? Enid looks quite a lot like her.'

That night they went to the tavern again and sat there till two in the morning when Aggie got off work.

'Are you out clean now?' Tucker's father said.

'Pretty much. But I still have to check in with the juvenile officer once a month wherever I decide to settle.'

'Where's that liable to be?'

'I'd like to go back to Underhill and find some work there. Thought maybe I could talk you into going with me.'

His father shook his head. 'There ain't nothing in Underhill, Roy. It's all done. The mines are played out and they won't let anybody cut the timber now. It's a graveyard, that place. No place for a young fella like you. No place for me either.'

'I just figured maybe we could find a place we could farm on shares and batch it together. Or Aggie could come along with us if she wanted to and keep house.'

'Not Aggie. She wouldn't leave Bluefield on a bet. She's got her sister here. And she makes steady money like I told you. Besides, Aggie needs a lot of people and commotion around her. She'd go nuts sitting on a dirt farm back in the hills someplace. And I wouldn't like it any better than she would, Roy. I had enough of that shit to last me a lifetime – outdoor crappers, hauling water, freezing your ass all winter, frying like a goddamned egg in a skillet from June to September – no sir, it ain't for me, not any more it ain't. Even if I could handle my end of the work I still wouldn't go for it. I got it licked here in Bluefield, Roy. I know when I'm well off.'

Tucker lay on a pallet in a corner of the room that night while his father and Aggie snored and snuffled in the bed. He lay awake for hours staring into the darkness, feeling the old house shudder when the wind came up, hearing it creak and moan.

At four in the morning he got up, found his clothes in the dark, put them on, crossed the room carrying his shoes, and let himself out into the upstairs hallway. He walked downstairs in his sock feet, then sat down and put on his shoes.

Forty minutes later, in a supermarket parking lot, he opened the hood of a black Chrysler sedan, jumped the wires, and started the engine. An hour or so after that, a state trooper pulled him over just south of Hinton and the following Thursday they took him back to the work farm.

PART TWO

CHAPTER SIXTEEN

THE BLUE LIMOUSINE pulled away from the arrival area at
Dulles, turned down the curving ramp and headed for the
exit, a uniformed man driving, Reser and Henemyer in
the back, behind a soundproof, bulletproof glass panel.
Easing on the expressway in the light, post–midnight
traffic, the car headed for downtown Washington.

'All right. Now he's got his two hundred thousand,'
Reser said. 'Do you think that'll hold him for a while?'

'I don't know. I can't guarantee what kind of a game
he's playing. I got the feeling he was testing us. Seeing
how far he could push.'

'Maybe we're borrowing trouble. When you look at it
logically, what does he have to gain by making a stink? He
can't blow the whistle on us without implicating himself.
He's no patriot. He admitted that in the note he sent us. I
mean he's not about to cut his own throat just to bring us
down, is he?'

'I don't know, I hope not. But if he's trying to get
even . . .'

'For what?'

'For his wife. That's the hang–up. That's what I see in
his face every time I talk to him.'

'He can't tie us to that. We know he didn't see it happen. Nobody saw it.'

'I know. That's what I told him. I told him that till I was
blue in the face. But he doesn't buy it.'

'You said he had a gun on you in Savannah. If all he wants is to get even why didn't he shoot you then?'

'I don't know. I guess he wasn't ready. Maybe he's still looking for some answers.'

'Jesus, he's got all the answers now. What else would he want to know?'

'I'm not sure. Maybe he wants to know who fingered him in the first place. There must be fifty thousand guys in jail in this country. You can bet Tucker would like to find out how we picked him.'

'You think that's why he's heading for Chicago?'

'It makes sense. According to Tagge, Applegate's the only guy he ever trusted.'

'That's all right,' Reser said. 'Let him look up Applegate. That'll keep him busy for a while. All we need is a couple more weeks. Just so we keep that little confession of his from floating into some newspaper office.'

'I've got an idea about that. What if we could fix it so it wouldn't hurt us even if he did release it?'

'There's no way to guarantee that.'

'I think maybe there is. I know a forger named Josh Hinkle. He's on parole. He won't talk because he can't afford to. He knows I could have him back in jail in twenty–four hours.'

'What's the connection?'

'This guy can duplicate any handwriting that's ever been invented, including Tucker's.'

'So what?'

'So we write up half a dozen conspiracy stories about Whittaker's death, implicating everybody we can think of. Castro, the Jewish Defence League, Goldwater, Reagan, the Teamsters, the Vatican, the more outlandish and far–fetched the better. But with the actual details, the helicopter and everything, exactly the same as in Tucker's version. We put these stories on the same kind of paper he used, then Xerox them the way he did. So even an expert would think that all the versions, including his, were written up by the same crank.'

'I think you've got something,' Reser said.

'As soon as we're ready, we mail out the first fake story. Then a different one every day for five or six days. We flood the media: networks, wire services, all the radio stations and newspapers, everybody – commentators and columnists – the whole works. It will be so crazy, such an onslaught, it will turn into a public scandal. And each mailing will come from a different city so it looks like an elaborate hoax. You see what I mean?'

'So if Tucker does get jumpy for some reason and sends out his story, nobody will give it a second look.'

'That's the idea,' Henemyer said.

'I think it's dynamite. How quick can you get started?'

'I'll contact Hinkle tonight and we'll start work tomorrow morning. We should have the first mailing ready in three or four days.'

CHAPTER SEVENTEEN

IT WAS SNOWING when Tucker's plane landed in Chicago, a light swirling snow, dancing and driving in the wind gusting off the lake. He took the airport bus to the Ambassador East, then walked south to Division Street and checked into a small residential hotel, the Bridgman, at the corner of Dearborn and Division.

As soon as he was inside his hotel room, he called Applegate's office. He got the answering service. 'Ask him to call Mr Brookshire at the Bridgman Hotel. It's important.'

He called the hospital then and was passed along to two different women. At last a man's voice came on and said Dr Applegate was out of the city.

'When do you expect him back?'

'I don't have that information.'

'I'm a friend of his from out of town. Do you know where I can reach him?'

'I'm afraid not.'

'You mean he's out of town but nobody knows where he is?'

'I mean *I* don't know where he is.'

When Tucker tried Applegate's home number in Oak Park, the operator came on and asked what number he was calling. When he told her she said, 'That number has been changed.'

'Can you give me the new number?'

'Just a moment.' There was a hollow silence at the other end of the line, a thin metallic click at regular intervals. Finally the operator came back on and said, 'I'm sorry. I can't give you the new number. It's unlisted.'

As soon as Tucker hung up his phone rang. 'There was a call for you while you were on the phone,' the hotel operator said, 'a Mr Applegate.'

'Did he leave a number?'

'No sir. He said he'd call again.'

'Yeah . . . all right. Let me talk to the bell captain.'

'Just a moment.'

When the bell desk answered, Tucker said, 'I have to rent a car.'

'There's an Avis garage three doors down on Dearborn.'

'Will you tell them I need a sedan, I don't care what make, with snow-tyres, or radials, something that won't get me stuck.'

'How long will you want it?'

'Maybe a week. Maybe longer.'

He opened the new bag he'd bought in Savannah and dumped it on the bed. Separating the two stuck–together pie tins, he took out the automatic, snapped in a clip, and put the gun in his jacket pocket. He put his clothes away,

64

then, in the dresser drawers, slid the bag into the closet, and lay down on the bed waiting for the phone to ring.

An hour later, at two-thirty in the afternoon, it rang. It was the bell captain. 'Your car's downstairs in the parking lot, Mr Brookshire. You can sign the papers when you come down.'

'I'll be right down.'

Tucker put on his jacket, went out into the hall, and pulled his room door shut behind him. As he started toward the elevator, he heard the phone ring in his room.

He had trouble unlocking the door. He wrenched and pulled, swearing under his breath, and counting the rings. On the seventh ring he finally got the door open. On the eighth ring he picked up the receiver.

'Yeah . . . hello . . .'

The voice at the other end sounded faint and muffled. 'Mr Brookshire?'

'Yes, this is . . . is that you, Bob?'

'Who is this?'

'It's Roy. Roy Tucker.' There was an empty silence at the other end. Then the line clicked and went dead.

'Bob . . .' Tucker jiggled the receiver and the city operator came on. 'I think I was cut off.'

'No, sir,' she said. 'Your party hung up.'

CHAPTER EIGHTEEN

AT THREE FORTY–FIVE that afternoon, Tucker was parked just down the street from Applegate's house. It was colder now, the snow had stopped, the wind had died down, and the air was clear and still.

At four–fifteen, a small blue bus, ELLIS DAY SCHOOL lettered on the side, pulled up in front of the house. Applegate's two daughters tumbled out, waving to their friends in the bus, and ran up the sidewalk to the front door. As they bounced up the steps to the porch, the door opened and a middle–aged black woman in a black dress with a white apron bustled them inside.

At five o'clock a brown Volvo station wagon stopped at the curb. Corinne Applegate got out and went into the house, a Norwich terrier trotting along beside her.

It got dark quickly then. But the street lamps lighted the front of Applegate's house. Tucker sat in the rented car, heater and radio on, watching the street and waiting. At seven–thirty Applegate still had not arrived.

At ten minutes to eight, Corinne Applegate came outside again, got into her car, and drove away. Half an hour later the downstairs lights went out and two windows lighted up on the second floor. At nine–thirty those lights went out. Then a light came on in a downstairs window at the back corner of the house, dim and flickering, somebody watching television. And the lights in the driveway and above the garage door buzzed and switched on.

At eleven–fifteen, Corinne Applegate's car came down the street and turned slowly into the driveway. When the garage doors lifted open, Tucker could see that the second space was empty. Applegate's car wasn't there.

Tucker waited till almost midnight. Then he got out of his car, crossed the street, climbed the steps to the porch, and rang the doorbell. He waited. No answer. He rang again. The porch light switched on then and he heard Corinne's voice, amplified and scratchy coming out of a small speaker beside the door. 'Who is it?'

Tucker turned his face towards the talk–back and said, 'It's Roy Tucker.'

'My God . . .'

'I have to see Bob.'

There was a long silence. Then, 'He's not here.'

'Then I have to see you.'

'I can't . . . I mean it's midnight . . .'

'It's important, Corinne. I mean it. If you don't open the door, I'll open it myself.'

When Corinne pulled the door open, the black woman was standing there too, just behind her. They both wore robes over their night clothes.

'You don't need a bodyguard or anything,' Tucker said. 'I'm not gonna hurt anybody.'

When they sat down in a small room to the left of the front hall, the black woman stood in the doorway.

'It's no skin off me,' Tucker said to Corinne, 'but your friend here is liable to hear some stuff you don't want her to know.'

'It's all right, Rosemary,' Mrs Applegate said. 'You can wait in the den.' They sat silent as the woman turned away, as her footsteps faded down the hallway. Then, 'Bob thinks you're dead.'

'No, he doesn't,' Tucker said, 'I talked to him this afternoon. And I talked to him when I was in Miami over a week ago.'

'I don't understand. He told me . . . I mean, all those stories in the paper . . .'

'I have to see him,' Tucker said.

'You can't. I mean he's not here.'

'Where is he?'

'Out of town.'

'Where?'

Trying to remember exactly what she'd been told to say, trying very hard not to make a mistake, she said, 'San Francisco . . . he arrives there tonight.' Picking up speed she said, 'That's where I went after dinner. I picked Bob up at the hospital and drove him to O'Hare.'

'Where's he staying in San Francisco?'

'I don't know. He wasn't sure.'

'You mean you don't know what hotel he's staying in?'

'It's the Clift, I think. Yes – that's right. He's at the Clift.'

For how long?'

'Five or six days.'

'He'll be back in Chicago in five or six days?'

'No. After he leaves San Francisco, he's going on to Seattle.'

'I just want to know when he'll be back here.'

'I'm not sure,' she said.

'Two weeks? Two months? Two years?' He sat there staring at her and she didn't answer. Finally he said, 'Why are you lying to me? I'm not some stranger off the street. Bob's the best friend I've got. The only one maybe. I don't understand what's going on.'

'I'm not lying,' she said weakly.

'Yes, you are and you know you are. But I can't figure out why. Ever since I got out of jail I've been trying to contact Bob. I don't want anything from him. I just need to talk to him. But he's nowhere to be found. He's out of the office, he's out of town, he's out of the country. When I get him on the phone, he hangs up. What does all that mean?'

'I don't know.'

'What's he scared of?'

'I don't know.'

'Is he scared of me?'

'I don't know.'

'Did he tell you I called him from Miami?'

'No. I told you before. Till you came to the door just now, I thought you were dead.'

They sat silent, then, in the dim–lit room. At last Tucker said, 'He's not in San Francisco, is he?'

'No.'

'Not in Seattle either?'

'No.'

'But you won't tell me where he is?'

'I can't,' she said.

'Jesus . . . I don't understand it. Why would he go to all this trouble?'

'I don't know. I don't know anything.'

CHAPTER NINETEEN

INJURED ON A night patrol north of Langbinh, Tucker first met Dr Applegate in the field hospital where the Red Cross helicopter delivered him.

Two months later, when Applegate was transferred to the recuperation centre in Osaka, he arranged for Tucker to be shipped there also, to finish up his tour of duty as an orderly.

Close to the same age but totally unlike in all other ways, they had become friends, cutting through the wall that separates officers from enlisted men, mostly because Applegate insisted on it.

For eight months, a little longer, they spent two or three hours together every day – Applegate, who was a good talker, talking most of the time, and Tucker, who was not a good talker at all, listening.

After three or four months had gone by, Tucker told him he'd been in prison. But it was nearly a year later, after they were both discharged and Applegate had brought Tucker home to spend some time in Oak Park with him and Corinne and the children, that he told him the complete truth, that until a judge in Wheeling had pressured him to enlist in the Army, he had been locked up in one jail or another for most of his adult life.

'Who cares?' Applegate said. 'You're not in jail now. And there's no reason why you ever should be again. You're a veteran with a good record and an honourable discharge. I'll manoeuvre you into a paramedic training programme and first thing you know you'll be all set. You'll have a profession and you'll be able to make some decent money.'

Months before, when they were still in Vietnam, Applegate had said, 'I'm a doctor. I'm a good one and I'm going to be better. But I've got some missionary blood in me. My wife says that's what I should have been . . . a missionary or a teacher or something. I don't believe that but I'll admit I like to fix things. And I like to fix people. I like to sew them up and set their broken bones and fix whatever else is ailing them. That's what I'm going to do to you, Tucker. I'm gonna fix you, whether you like it or not. I'm gonna pull rank on you and teach you a different way to think. When I get finished with you, you'll have a whole new idea of what you're worth, of what Roy Tucker's all about.'

Later on, when they were stationed in Japan, Applegate said one day, 'Let's take me, for instance. We could take somebody else for instance, but then I wouldn't have a chance to talk about myself. Like I told you once before I was born with a silver spoon in my mouth. A big spoon. Pure silver. I mean the doors never squeaked in our house. They didn't dare. My great–grandfather was the richest man in Atlanta and he married the richest lady in Macon. Their son, Amos, my grandfather, married the richest lady in Mobile, and my father, Robert Kenneth Applegate Senior, married the second–richest girl in Providence, Rhode Island. Broke out of the South and turned into a Yankee.

'What I'm saying is . . . a lot of my problems were solved the day I was born. Since I didn't have to work at anything, I was free to work at whatever I wanted to. I went to Choate and Princeton and had a fine old time. And when I decided I wanted to be a doctor, I went to Harvard Medical School. It never occurred to me that I could fail at anything. So I didn't fail. All the right doors swung open and I went strolling through.

'There's a point to all this, Roy. I'm not just telling you what a hot shot I am. There is, as they say, a moral to the story – also a twist, a little wrinkle. I mean when somebody says we're not all created equal, nobody with horse sense can argue with that. Some people are very smart or extremely beautiful. Or they can run fast or make people laugh. So those people have a head start, no question about it. And I had a head start. Lots of good things were handed to me.

'So what's my point? The point is this: the sharpest guy in my class at Choate was a black kid named Regis Smithers from Red Hook, one of the lousiest sections in Brooklyn. He had nine brothers and sisters, all from different fathers. And none of those fathers ever showed up at the house much. His mother was a pusher, his two brothers were addicts, and all his sisters were hookers. And Regis was arrested a dozen times before he was fourteen. So what happened? Some lady in juvenile court had him tested and found out how smart he was. She took him over and turned him around. He ended up with a scholarship to Choate and a scholarship to Brown. And when he was twenty–four he started his own company, manufacturing computer components. Last year he sold out to Texaco for thirty–seven million dollars. Now he lives in a big estate in Harrison, New York. He's married to Paul Robeson's great–niece, has three nice kinds, and he's got a great life. Handles all his investments on the telephone, plays tennis every afternoon, and smiles a lot. Brushes his teeth with Dom Perignon, I'll bet.

'Case history number two. Princeton. My class valedictorian, Phi Beta Kappa his junior year, was Fred Buchanan. Fred was an orphan, grew up in a Baptist foundling home in Lexington, Kentucky. Not a very good student but a good track man. Threw the discus and the javelin. So some alumni group wangled him a scholarship to Princeton. As soon as he got there, something clicked. He started to study, made good grades, and ended up making better grades than anybody. During his senior year he got a brainstorm and started an insurance company, did a snow job on somebody at Continental Life, and they took him on as a subsidiary, a one–man operation, selling low–cost life insurance to college students. He was a millionaire before he was twenty–six and ten years later he was president of five insurance companies.

'You get my point, Roy? I'm not talking about getting rich, or being rich. I'm talking about the way things happen. And there's two sides to the story – at least two. The smartest and richest and handsomest guy in my class at medical school is serving two years in federal prison for Medicare fraud. He didn't need the money. He just wanted it. And Robin Settle, my room mate at Choate, hung himself in a prison in Turkey after they caught him with a kilo of cocaine in his Gucci suitcase. Okay? I told you there was a moral. Here's the moral. When somebody tells you he can't make it because the cards are stacked against him, when somebody tells you he can't miss because he's holding all the cards, I say both those guys are full of shit. You know what I mean?'

'I know what you think you mean,' Tucker said.

'You think I'm wrong?'

'I know you're wrong. I knew guys in West Virginia that were heading for the junk yard from the minute they were born. I saw guys in jail that if you offered them gold in one hand and horse shit in the other they'd take the horse shit every time. And there were guys in my outfit in Vietnam that if one good thing ever happened to them, they'd be too dumb or too stoned or too drunk to know it. You're talking about people that want good stuff. I'm talking about people who've never seen it, who wouldn't know something good if it fell on them. Those are the people *I* know.'

'Are you telling me that's the way you are?'

'I'm not talking about myself at all. I'm just saying that's what I know. That's what I'm used to.'

CHAPTER TWENTY

THE MORNING AFTER he talked with Corinne Applegate, Tucker got up early, ate breakfast in the coffee shop downstairs, and drove down to the corner of State and Ohio Streets.

In the lobby of an office building there, on the northeast corner of the intersection, he checked the tenant directory, referring to a page he'd torn out of the classified phone book.

Taking the elevator to the fifth floor he found the door he was looking for. In black letters on the glass it said, WICKWIRE AND SUSKI – INVESTIGATIONS.

Harold Wickwire was a slight man, thinning hair, pale skin, and brown eyes, his clothing plain and monochromatic. Cream–coloured suit, tan shirt, olive drab tie, brown shoes – he seemed to be, in some way, war surplus. His office was neat and orderly, only a small note pad on his glass–topped desk beside the telephone, nothing at all on top of the two metal file cabinets – no flowers or books or magazines, no mementoes, no family pictures. Tucker felt, sitting across from him, that if an eviction notice came, Wickwire could clear out in seven minutes.

Wickwire sat looking at a small piece of note paper Tucker had given him; he studied it thoroughly, looking up occasionally with clouded eyes. Finally he said, 'Did someone recommend us to you?'

'No. I found your name in the phone book. I'm staying at a hotel on Division Street and your office was the closest one I could find. Most of the other guys who do your kind of work are down in the Loop.'

Wickwire studied the paper again. Then, 'Let's go over this a little bit, Mr Brookshire. You want us to locate a missing person. Dr Robert Applegate. Is that what it amounts to?'

'I don't know if you'd call him a missing person. I think his wife knows where he is. But she won't say anything. At least she won't tell me. At first she said he was out of town but I knew that wasn't the truth.'

'Why would she lie about it?'

'I don't know. I guess he told her to.'

'Why would he do that?'

'I don't know. That's what I want to find out.'

'Why do you think he's avoiding you?'

'I don't know. We're good friends. He's my best friend.'

'When did you see him last?' Wickwire said.

'I don't know. A few years.'

When Wickwire's eyes came up and questioned that, Tucker said, 'I've been out of the country.'

'When did you actually talk to him last?'

'I called him from Miami a week or so ago. And I called his office yesterday.'

'What did he say?'

'Nothing much. We only talked for a minute. He took my number and said he'd call me back. But I never heard from him. That was the Miami call. Yesterday he just hung up.'

'Do you mind telling me why you are so keen to see Dr Applegate?'

'I told you. I want to talk to him. We're friends.'

'But he doesn't want to talk to you. Doesn't sound like such a good friend.'

Tucker stood up, reached across the desk and picked up the piece of note paper. 'I think we'd better forget it. I told you what I want and I gave you the particulars. If you don't want to do it, I'll go downtown and find somebody who does.'

'I just asked why you wanted . . .'

'None of your business.'

'It could be my business if Applegate turns up dead in a day or so.'

'You think I'm crazy enough to give you my name and address and show you my driver's licence if I'm planning to knock over somebody? Look . . . we've got a simple problem here. Do you want the job or don't you?'

Wickwire, unruffled, said, 'I think we'll be able to handle it. Our fees are one–fifty a day plus expenses. Three hundred minimum down payment. The balance payable before we turn over the information to you.'

Tucker sat down and took out Brookshire's traveller's cheques. 'I'll give you a hundred–dollar bonus if I hear from you by tomorrow noon.'

'Fair enough.'

'And I'll tell you right now, you won't get any help from his office or the hospital. Your best bet is to tail his wife.'

'That's what I plan to do.'

CHAPTER TWENTY–ONE

AN HOUR LATER, in a small bleak apartment in a dingy section of Maywood, a suburb due west of Oak Park, Applegate and Corinne sat across from each other at the kitchen table.

'Here's what I want you to do. Call Factor and tell him to open up the lake house.'

'Oh, Bob, for God's sake. Please . . .'

'Tell him I'll be up there day after tomorrow.'

'What is going through your head? I just don't understand you.'

'We were going there for Christmas week anyway. I'm just going up early, that's all.'

'Oh, honey, what are you so afraid of?'

'I'm not afraid. It's not a question of that. I'm just trying to handle a bad situation.'

'What situation? What can Roy do to you? I talked to him. He's no different than he ever was. He just wants to see you. Wouldn't that be simpler than hiding here in this crummy apartment or running to Wisconsin to lock yourself up in the lake house?'

'Use your head, Corinne. We can't pretend that Roy is the same guy I knew before. Too much has happened. When he killed Bert Riggins . . .'

'You were never sure he did that.'

'I didn't want to think he did it. But the jury thought he did. That's the main thing. And according to the papers

76

he killed somebody else, another prisoner, after they broke out of jail in October. And maybe he was involved in Whittaker's assassination. That's what the papers say now.'

'The papers also said he was killed up in Canada. So maybe they're wrong about the other stuff too.'

'Maybe they are. But until I know for sure, I can't afford . . .'

'Can't afford what?'

'I don't know. God knows what's in Roy's head, what kind of craziness he's mixed up with.'

'He doesn't act crazy. He's a lot more calm than you are, I'll tell you that.'

'Jesus, Corinne, will you stop fighting me on this? Just trust me.'

'I'm trying to. But you don't make sense. It's not like you to want to run off and hide.'

'I don't want to. But I think it's the only thing to do.'

'What about me and the girls?'

'He won't bother you. Tucker's not interested in anything but me right now. I'm the one he wants to see.'

'But you can't stay up there at the lake forever.'

'I won't have to. He'll get tired of waiting around. By the time we come home after Christmas he'll be gone. I'm sure of it.'

'What if he's not?'

'He will be.'

She sat silent for a long time looking down at her empty coffee cup. Finally he said, 'What's the matter?'

'I was just thinking about when you brought him home with you from Vietnam. Do you remember what I said?'

'You said I was crazy.'

'No, I didn't. I said you were bucking ridiculous odds. I said you couldn't take a grown–up man with no education, a man who'd spent most of his life in jail, and turn him into a different person.'

'But I could have. It would have worked. He had everything he needed except for one thing. He didn't believe in himself. He had no self–confidence.'

77

'It didn't work, Bob. That's all I'm saying. But you still believed in him. Even after he took off without saying goodbye or thank you or anything. And when we finally heard about him again, when they arrested him for killing Bert Riggins, you were Johnny–on–the–spot. You got Schnaible to defend him, you testified as a character witness, you stuck with him when nobody else would give him a second look.'

'I know what you're saying,' Applegate said. 'If I could go out of my way to help him before, why can't I at least talk to him now. Is that it?'

'Something like that.'

'I can't, Corinne. It just wouldn't work. Things are different now. He's trouble and I don't need that kind of trouble. *We* don't need it.'

CHAPTER TWENTY–TWO

AFTER HE LEFT Wickwire's office, Tucker drove east on Ohio Street to Lake Shore Drive, then north along the lake, past Evanston, Wilmette, Winnetka, Glencoe, and Highland Park. When he came to Lake Forest he turned off the Drive and drove slowly through the maze of walled estates and solid homes, gates and wide lawns, long curving driveways and five–car garages.

When he came to Riggins' house he parked across the street and sat looking at it for a long time. Brick and timber and a steep–pitched slate roof, leaded windows, and the apartment where he'd slept, in the back over the garage. He could see it all from the street. Tucker got out of the car and crossed the street for a closer look. On the gate post there was a small sign with the name of a real estate company. Above the name it said, *Offered by* and at the bottom there was a telephone number.

While he was looking at the sign, not seeing it really, his mind wandering, a grey–haired man in a blue mackinaw wearing a fur hat, walked down the driveway to the gate. 'Not quite so cold today,' he said.

'No, it's not. Still cold enough though.'

'Anything I can do for you?'

'No, I don't think so. I was . . . I was just trying to locate some people I know. I thought maybe this was their house but I guess I was wrong.'

'Nobody living here now. This place has been vacant for four or five months. Who were the people you were looking for? I've spent most of my life here in Lake Forest. I might know them.'

'Uh . . . Johnson,' Tucker said. 'A man named Bruce Johnson and his family. He's a cousin of mine.'

'Johnson? Well, there are plenty of Johnsons on the north shore. It's a Swede name. Lots of Swedes settled around Chicago. But I don't remember any Johnson ever living here in the Riggins' place.'

'Is he the owner?'

'Used to be. He's dead now. The last six years or so the house has changed hands at least four times. I know because every time somebody moves out the real estate people move me in. To look after the place till they find a buyer. It's a funny thing. Riggins lived here for twenty–five years. Now they can't get anybody to stay for more than a year and a half. I guess you're not from around here, are you?'

'No, I'm not.'

'If you were, most likely you'd have heard about Riggins. He was murdered. His own chauffeur killed him. Drove him down to Indianapolis one day for some reason or other and while they were staying there in a motel, this

79

chauffeur gave Riggins a dynamite shot of morphine. Killed him deader than hell. It turned out that this guy and Riggins' wife had a romance going and the old man was in the way. Same old story. But they both went to the pen for it. People never learn, do they?'

Driving back to Chicago, a fog starting to roll in now off Lake Michigan, Tucker thought about what the house guard had said. It had sounded like a clipping from an old newspaper, memorised, a cut and dried, fourth–hand version of something that had happened to strangers a long time ago.

After his post–Vietnam stay at Applegate's house in Oak Park, Tucker had gone straight to Riggins, had answered a classified ad in the *Tribune*, and had been hired at once.

'I've got three cars,' Riggins said. 'As long as they look good and run good, as long as you drive the way I tell you to and don't try to dick me around on gas and oil and garage bills, we'll get along fine. But if you try to fuck me up, I'll shut your water off good.'

Tucker told him he'd been in prison before he enlisted in the Army. He volunteered the information. 'Why are you telling me that?' Riggins asked.

'I figured I ought to tell you the truth. Just in case it makes a difference to you.'

'Makes no difference at all. I like to hire people nobody else wants. Gives me an edge. You know what I mean?'

'Yes, sir.'

'The only thing that scares me is when a man is too honest. Then I start to think he's not honest at all. I never trust a policeman or a priest or a judge or an old lady in a Salvation Army uniform. Professional Christers. Can't trust any of those assholes.'

Tucker worked six months for Riggins before he had any conversation at all with Thelma. She never seemed to leave the house without Riggins, never asked to be driven anywhere by herself.

She was little and thin and ill–at–ease. Whenever she went somewhere in the car with Riggins, he seemed dissatisfied with what she was wearing. 'Go to Saks. Go to Bonwits. Get yourself some decent clothes. You look like the housekeeper going to the movies on her day off.'

'I don't like those stores,' Thelma said. 'I don't like the people that work there. They're all snooty women, wearing too much perfume and looking down their noses at me.'

'Speak up, for Christ's sake. Tell them who you are. You're the customer. It's my money. They're supposed to do what you tell them.'

'I can't do that. I don't like to boss people around.'

One summer day, hot and muggy, Tucker was washing the cars, wearing jeans, barefoot with his shirt off. He looked up and Thelma was standing in the doorway to the garage.

'It's awful hot out here,' she said. 'I thought maybe you'd like to come into the kitchen and drink a glass of iced tea.' She was wearing a cotton dress and sandals. She looked sixteen years old.

'I don't think I'd better. I've got a lot to do.'

He'd never seen her smile before. 'Just let it go,' she said. 'That's what everybody else is doing. Soon as Bert goes out of town for a few days everything slows down considerably around here. I guess nobody's afraid of me the way they are with him. Come on. I made the iced tea myself. It'll taste good to you.'

When they were sitting at the staff dining–table in one corner of the big bright kitchen, Tucker said, 'Where is everybody?'

'Well, Bert's up in Canada trying to catch a fish. You already know that. The cook is watching television with the housekeeper. And the maid is out in the greenhouse making goo–goo eyes at the gardener.'

After she refilled his glass she said, 'I've been wanting to talk to you for a long time. Bert says you're from West Virginia but he didn't know what part.'

'Underhill's where I was born. You probably never heard of it.'

'I guess not. What's it near?'

'Elkins. Not far from Elkins.'

'I know Elkins. We used to visit right close to there. Mom had second cousins who lived outside Redhouse.'

'That's not far from us. Just up 219 from Elkins. We used to play baseball on Sundays sometimes up at Redhouse.'

Thelma came from North Carolina, a town in the west end of the state called Hazelwood. Her father ran a country store. 'We were six kids, five of us girls, only a year or so apart in age all the way down the line. It was a big load on Dad's shoulders, trying to keep all of us fed and looking nice. So I went into Asheville, soon as I was out of high school, and found me a job at the F. W. Woolworth store. Then a girl I met there, Rosalie Veach, found out about a radio factory up in Knoxville that was looking for girls to do assembly work. So we went on up there, the two of us, and lived together for a year or so till Rosalie got married. The next thing I knew I was here in Chicago. And I got a shock, I'll tell you. I found out there's more North Carolina people up here than there is in North Carolina. I mean it. At least it seems that way. Just look at you – from West Virginia. Who would ever think that two people who know about those Sunday ball games at Redhouse would run into each other in fancy–pants Lake Forest?'

She had worked as a waitress in Evanston, then at a coffee shop in Glencoe. Riggins had seen her there and had sent his housekeeper to persuade her to come to work for him.

'She offered me a lot more money than I was making, and my meals besides, and a nice room with a colour TV in a big fine house, so I thought, "Why not? I'll try it for three months or so." As it turned out it was less than three months. By then Bert and I were married. That was what he'd had in mind right along.'

After that first afternoon they talked for a few minutes every day or so, usually when Tucker was working in the garage. One day Thelma said, 'I don't know why Bert wanted to marry me. I honestly don't. I mean he's an older man, been everywhere, successful. He could have any woman he wanted, I guess. You should see the pictures of his other wives. One of them was an actress even. I never knew what he wanted with a down–home runt like me. I still don't.'

Listening to her, Tucker remembered Riggins saying, 'I like to hire people nobody else wants. It gives me an edge. You know what I mean?'

Driving south toward Chicago now, Tucker tried to sort through the pieces of the hours and days he remembered, tried to pinpoint the moment when he and Thelma had changed direction, when Riggins stopped being his employer and her husband and became, clearly and finally, the enemy.

It was an impossible process, attempting to freeze time, isolate words and thoughts and impulses. Nonetheless, realising it might not be the answer, not the total answer surely, Tucker settled in on a tiny sliver of an autumn afternoon when Thelma had said, 'I don't belong here. You don't either. We're strangers at the picnic. There's nothing here for people like us.'

CHAPTER TWENTY–THREE

'I GET UP in the morning,' Thelma said. 'I look at myself in the glass and I don't know who I am. Silk nightgowns with lace on them, gold–plated faucets in the bathroom, breakfast on a tray in my bed whether I want it or not – I don't know what to do with all this fancy business. I can't handle it. I read in the magazines where everybody's supposed to be concerned with their conveniences and comforts, trying to move up all the time, trying to get to the point where they don't have to do anything for themselves, where there's some machine or some servant to do it all. Well, that's what it's like for me. I've got nothing to do. I'm not allowed to do anything: can't cook, can't clean, can't even wash out my own clothes. I'm treated like some kind of a cripple, and I hate it.

'When I think about how it was at home, the thing I remember most is Mom and my sisters and me all working together around the house – cleaning, doing the wash, cooking supper, baking bread and angel–food cakes, frying side–meat, cranking the ice-cream freezer till our arms about dropped off. Or we'd all sit and sew together of an afternoon when the light was good, laughing and joking and our fingers flying. The bunch of us could hem up curtains or dish towels so fast you wouldn't believe it. Or make rag rugs, or samplers to hang on the wall. And my dad and my brother always had more hand–knit sweaters than they knew what to do with. The Chester women were well thought of as cooks and for their needlework. Everybody in the township knew about us.'

It was this nostalgia for another life, the longing–back to a different place, that pulled Thelma toward Tucker. She needed to talk about North Carolina to someone who knew the language of the hills, needed to see his eyes respond, the slow smile, the head nodding in affirmation. Tucker knew the land she longed for. Seeing him, talking with him, convinced her that it would still be there when she went back.

Beyond that, beyond her need to reassure herself that there was still a life for her outside and beyond the walls of money that surrounded Lake Forest, she told herself that she had no interest in Roy Tucker, and in the beginning it was true. They were fellow victims, victimised in different ways by the same man.

Each of them recognised their weaknesses in the other,

the same hesitations, the same lack of self–esteem, the same fears. Even if they had been irresistibly drawn to each other, tormented by physical desire, neither of them would have had the courage to deceive Bert Riggins in his own home, in the apartment over the garage, or in one of his cars parked on some Illinois side road.

Their common roots pulled them slowly together. Their common fear of Riggins kept them apart. With no inclination to become lovers, they became friends. In fifteen– and twenty–minute isolated fragments of time they came at last to know each other, to depend on those short conversations, to look forward to them.

Tucker told her, bit by bit, about his sister in Canada, about his mother's death, about his forlorn one–armed father. And for the first time he managed to express his feelings about life in prison, how he detested it and how, for many years, he had needed it, how it had given him an identity he had been unable to find on the outside, shored him up, defined him, provided him rotten refuge from a world he couldn't deal with.

She in turn told him every detail of her blameless life – full–scale portraits of her parents, her brother, and her sisters, tales from her schooldays, stories about the jobs she had held, friends she'd made, people she'd worked with. And one afternoon, at last, she came to the apartment over the garage, and told Tucker about Riggins, all the unsettling ugliness.

'There's something sick about him. Something mean and twisted. I read someplace that a man who washes his hands all the time is full of meanness. Inside they feel guilty for all the orneriness they've done to other people and they're trying to wash it away. I don't know if that's true or not but if it's true then Riggins must be the guiltiest bastard who ever drew a breath. Because he never stops cleaning himself. Did you ever notice how often he changes clothes? When he's at home he changes everything, from the skin out, three or four times a day. And every time he changes he takes a shower bath, powders himself up good, and sprinkles himself with some kind of

French toilet water. His hair's so thin you could practically count every hair, but all the same he shampoos it twice a day. And he shaves morning and afternoon. And usually again before he goes to bed.

'He gets manicures and pedicures at least once a week and in between times he's always clipping and filing away at himself. And trimming his eyebrows with little scissors. And the hairs in his nose and ears. He brushes his teeth and gargles Listerine every time he passes a bathroom. And he carries eyedrops with him in his pocket. And nose drops. Always squirting something into his eyes or his nose. And he's all the time cleaning out his ears with cotton swabs and alcohol.

'The same stuff goes on when he's down in the Loop at his office. That's what his secretary told me. He's got a big bathroom and a closet full of clothes there, too, and he never stops washing up and putting on clean duds.

'When I was first married to him I thought it was funny. I'd never seen a man so particular about himself. Never heard of a man who wasn't a sissy sprucing himself up from morning till night like a silly old woman. But after a while it didn't seem funny to me anymore. I can't explain it but there was something scary about it. Like I said, like somebody trying to wash something terrible off their hands. And the better I got to know Bert, the more I knew about him, the stranger it all seemed to me.

'He likes to tell me about all the things he gets away with in his business. How he manipulates people and swindles big companies and cheats on his taxes. Most times it's not even a big deal, just some little mean thing he's done to somebody, but his eyes get all funny when he tells me about it, like it's the most important, exciting thing he's ever done in his life.

'I told you before I don't know why he wanted to marry me. And I don't. But sometimes I think it's because he needed somebody around all the time, some dumb bunny like me who couldn't hurt him in any way, who couldn't do anything except sit there and listen. The talking is the best part for him, telling about himself – what he said and what he did, who he did it to, what they said, all the crummiest little facts and details.'

'I wish you wouldn't tell me all this stuff,' Tucker said. 'I'm just working here. It's none of my business. Why are you blurting out everything to me?'

She started to cry then. 'Because I have to tell somebody. Because if I don't have a friend or anybody I can talk to a little bit, they'll have to put me in the booby hatch. I'm like a prisoner here. Don't you know that? You think I haven't tried to leave him? I've tried, all right. Three times the first month we were married.'

'If you hate him so much, why'd you . . .'

'Don't even say it. I married him because I was young and dumb and scared. And because he fooled me. I never cared anything about him, not in any man and woman way, but he was good to me. Treated me like a human being, soft–spoken and sweet, like somebody's uncle. That's why I married him – not because of the money. I thought I'd have some peace and a clean place to live in, and a decent man who wouldn't mistreat me. Sounds crazy now but it meant something then. I really meant to be a good wife. I had nothing but good intentions towards him. But they didn't last long. He saw to that. We hadn't been married a week when he sashayed in here one night with a big yellow–haired woman in a fur coat, the two of them all full of jokes and wisecracks and smelling like a saloon.'

'What did you do?'

'I tried to be nice. I didn't know who the woman was. If she was a business person or what. But it didn't take me long to get the drift of things. The woman was a call girl or a hooker or whatever you want to call her. And Bert's idea was that the three of us would go to bed together. "Angela's nice," he said to me. "You'll like Angela as much as I do. And I can see already that she likes you." Well, I'll tell you, I was so shook up I didn't know what to do. So I just ran down the hall to one of the guest rooms, locked myself in and stayed there all night. Bert thought it was funny. Next morning I thought he'd laugh himself sick about it.

'Anyway, he kept trying to get me involved whenever he came home late at night with some bimbo he'd picked up. But I took to locking myself in as soon as I heard him turn in the driveway. If he was by himself I'd come out. If he had some floozy with him I stayed out of sight.'

'Why didn't you just take off?'

'You think I didn't try? I told you. Three times the first few months we were married. And half a dozen times since then. But he always finds me and brings me back. You can do anything you want to when you've got money.'

'Like hell you can,' Tucker said. 'He can't just keep you like a dog on a leash if you don't want to stay around.'

'He can't, huh? That's what you think. That's all you know.'

She sat in a big chair by the window in Tucker's apartment, her feet tucked up under her, her handkerchief a damp ball in her hand. She looked tiny and helpless and wounded. Tucker walked across the room, stood beside her and put his hand on her shoulder. As soon as he touched her she started to cry again. He knelt down on the floor beside her and put his arm around her shoulders. 'Don't cry like that,' he said, 'I hate to see you cry.' But she couldn't stop. She held on to the front of his jacket with both hands and pressed her face against his chest. At last both his arms went around her and he could feel how small and thin she was under her sweater. Two months later Riggins was dead and a few weeks after that both Tucker and Thelma were in prison.

CHAPTER TWENTY–FOUR

DAN RATHER'S FACE on television, a final editorial comment on the evening news.

'A strange postscript to the death of Ex–President Neal Whittaker. In an atmosphere of genuine sorrow and national loss, some group or some individual has decided, it seems, that any occasion, however tragic, can be used as a springboard for a prank, for some elaborate joke, something to amuse the sick minds that seem always to be with us. Here's what's happening. On three separate occasions in the last few days, the newspapers and magazines, the radio and television stations around the country, have been swamped with copies of what seems to be a hand-written insider's confession, the complete story of who was responsible for President Whittaker's death, who took part in the conspiracy. So far the list of names revealed as conspirators reads like a who's who of national and, in some cases, international political life. Each new arrival in the mail, always the same handwriting, details a different conspiracy and a different list of conspirators. We will not dignify this insane scheme by revealing any of the specifics. But we do feel that some comment must be made. Again we say that a society that tries to solve political problems with bullets, a society that becomes callous to the idea of assassination, accepts it as a fact of political life, even finds some perverse humour in it . . .'

'What do you think?' Henemyer said, switching off the television set.

'So far so good,' Reser said. They were in Reser's office in the executive office building, opposite end of the tunnel from the White House. 'That's the reaction we wanted. But let's not celebrate too soon. I'm always leery of an operation that goes without a hitch.'

'Not me. That's the kind I like.'

'That's because you're young and innocent.' He lit a cigarette and tilted back in his chair. 'What's Tucker up to?'

'Still in Chicago. Still trying to contact Applegate. No luck so far.'

'Who's doing the leg work for us out there?'

'Local people. We don't want anybody from Washington involved if we don't have to.'

'What did you tell them?'

'The usual. National security. I asked for general surveillance on Tucker and I'm getting it. They think his name is Brookshire. They don't know who he is. When he leaves Chicago, we'll use the Bureau if we have to. Stokely will okay the donkey work for us, no questions asked.'

'Are you sure there's no problem with Applegate? He was Tagge's man. He's an unknown quantity as far as I'm concerned.'

'No problem. He doesn't know anything. He just knows pieces.'

'Maybe so. But according to Tagge he's a shrewd son–of–a–bitch. You can bet he knows what to do with two and two.'

'If Tucker doesn't get to him, there'll be no problem.'

'What if Tucker does get to him?'

'Then we'll make some adjustments.'

CHAPTER TWENTY-FIVE

TUCKER SIGNED THREE traveller's cheques and passed them across the desk to Wickwire who checked the signatures and the date, fastened the cheques together with a paper clip, and slipped them into his desk drawer.

'Maywood,' he said then. 'It's the first suburb west of Oak Park. The street is Kingstree. The number is 877. Applegate's on the third floor. Apartment 3G. But I don't think he'll be there long. Unless I miss my guess he'll be making a move today.'

Two hours later, eleven-thirty in the morning, Tucker walked down the third floor corridor of the building on Kingstree Street, found the apartment he was looking for, and rang the bell. A long, insistent ring. Then he bent over and slipped a folded sheet of paper under the door.

Inside the apartment Applegate came out of the bed-room and stood in the centre of the living room looking at the door, at the piece of paper just inside it on the floor. The doorbell sounded again. Applegate walked quietly to the door, bent over and picked up the folded note, opened it and read it.

I have to see you, Bob. I know you're in there. I'm going to wait outside till you let me in. I don't care how long it takes.

                                                        Roy Tucker

Applegate stood with his hands at his sides. The doorbell sounded three more times. At last he reached out, snapped the dead bolt, and opened the door.

Tucker stood in the doorway. 'What's going on, Bob? What the hell is going on?'

Applegate motioned him in and closed the door behind him. 'What do you mean?'

'What do you think I mean? I've been breaking my ass to get in touch with you. Finally I get you on the phone, you say you'll call me back, and that's the last I hear of you. Next time I get you on the phone you hang up.'

'What did you think I was going to do? What do you expect? Don't you think I read the papers? You know what they're saying about you. They think maybe you killed Whittaker.'

'I did.'

'Jesus Christ.'

'I didn't have any choice. They had Thelma. They said they'd kill her if I didn't do what they wanted. They meant it. They would have killed her. And finally they did. But by then it was too late. I'd already done what they wanted me to.'

'What do you mean, they? Who are they?'

'I don't know. I mean I know some names and some faces but that's all. I didn't know who was giving the orders or why they wanted to kill Whittaker. I still don't – not for sure. That's why I was trying so hard to get in touch with you. That's why I wrote you that letter from Costa Rica. I thought maybe you could help me. Or at least you'd know what happened in case they killed me too.'

'I told you before. I never got a letter from you.'

'I sent it registered. To your house in Oak Park.'

'It didn't come.'

Tucker took two folded Xerox pages out of his jacket pocket and handed them to Applegate. 'Read this. It's all I know about what happened.'

Applegate sat down on the couch and read the two pages, Tucker in the armchair facing him.

Finally Applegate looked up and said, 'Jesus . . . I can't believe it.'

'It's all true, Bob. Just the way it happened.'

'They didn't tell you what they wanted you to do?'

'No. I knew it was something lousy but I didn't know what. All I knew was I was going to get to be with Thelma again. They promised me a house of my own down in Costa Rica. And money in the bank. But most of all I'd be out of jail and Thelma and I could live some kind of life together.'

'What was that story about you being killed up in Canada?'

'That was their original plan, I think. That was supposed to be me. But I outmanoeuvred them. I made them fly Thelma and me back to Costa Rica. So they shot some other poor bastard up in Canada and pretended it was me.'

'What was the point of that?'

'Cover–up. The same as always. They closed the case, stopped questions, put a lid on everything. The people say to themselves, "Roy Tucker shot Whittaker and the police killed Tucker. So that takes care of that." It's all neat and finished now. Except it's not because I don't want it to be.'

Applegate sat silent for a long moment. Then he handed the folded pages back to Tucker and said, 'Can I give you some advice?'

'Sure.'

'Do you need money?'

'No. I've got cash and a bunch of traveller's cheques. And a big cashier's cheque.'

'Then disappear. That's my advice.'

'No good, Bob. I can't do that.'

'You can't do anything else. You're bucking something you can't handle. It's scary. They'll squash you like a bug whenever they're ready. You know that, don't you?'

'Sure I do. They've already tried. But I'm hard to kill.'

Applegate shook his head. 'Go to New Orleans or Montreal. Mexico City even. Someplace where nobody knows you. Change your name and forget about everything that's happened.'

'What about Thelma? Do I forget what happened to her?'

'You have to.'

'No, I don't, Bob. I don't want to and I can't. They ran her down like she was some stray dog on the highway. Slammed her against a stone wall and kept right on going. You think I can forget that?'

'You have to.'

'Who says so? There isn't any law for these pricks. They're outside the law. They do whatever they damned well please.'

'That's what I mean. That's what I'm trying to tell you. You're one guy by yourself. Sometimes you have to admit you're licked. All of us do.'

'Not me. Not by those bastards. There's a guy named Henemyer. And another one named Reser. They think they've got me one foot in the grave already. But they're wrong. Those two guys are gonna wish they'd never heard of Thelma. They'll be sorry they ever laid eyes on me.'

'You're crazy, Roy. They'll have you killed by somebody you've never seen before. Some guy will walk up to you on the street and blow a hole in you before you even know what's going on.'

'Maybe, but I don't think so.' He grinned then. 'I've got an edge on them, Bob. They can't kill me. I'm already dead.'

CHAPTER TWENTY–SIX

AFTER THE JURY came back into the Indianapolis court-room that afternoon five years earlier, after the judge had sentenced Tucker to prison for the murder of Riggins and sentenced Thelma for complicity, after they were allowed to be married by a justice of the peace in an anteroom off the mess hall in the Marion County Jail, they were led to a visitor's room and permitted to spend twenty minutes together, across the table from each other, the guard tilted back in his chair thirty feet away.

Thelma sat silent, her eyes down, her hand holding Tucker's on the table top. Finally he said, 'You'd better say something or first thing you know the time will be up and it'll be too late.' She looked up then, her eyes filled with tears. 'Cut that out,' he said. 'What have you got to cry about? I agreed to marry you, didn't I? Went through the ceremony and everything. Twenty or thirty women just dying to be Mrs Roy Tucker and you turned out to be the lucky one. I'm surprised you're not singing at the top of your lungs and dancing around the room.'

'He gave you such an awful sentence. I never thought it would be so long. I wish you could take my sentence and I could take yours.'

'What good would that do?'

'I don't know. I just hate to think . . .'

'You shouldn't have been on trial even. You didn't do anything.'

'They thought I did. That's all that counts.'

'You shouldn't have said what you did. When you said you were glad he's dead . . .'

'I meant it. It's the truth. You know how he treated me, how he treated everybody. Anybody who likes to hurt people the way he did . . .' She started to cry then, dropped her head on her arms and sobbed. The guard looked up, then went back to the magazine he was reading.

'Cut it out,' Tucker said. 'Nobody wants to see you bawling and moaning and getting a red nose. People will think you're sorry you married me.' He handed her his handkerchief. 'Come on, honey. I don't want to talk about Riggins. We don't have to worry about him or talk about him anymore.'

She blew her nose and dabbed at her eyes with the handkerchief.

'That's better,' he said. 'That's more like it. With a good-looking husband like me, you've got to stay on your toes, keep up with the competition, you know what I mean?'

She looked up at him and managed the beginning of a smile.

'It's good that you'll be getting out before I do,' he said. 'I like the idea. You can find a good job and save your money, buy us a nice house and a car, a couple of television sets and a deep freeze, stuff like that. And a nice soft bed. Then I'll have a decent place to come to without any worries about where my next meal is coming from.'

They were silent again for a long hollow moment. Finally she said, 'I wish you'd have told me what you were fixing to do. I wish you'd have talked to me about it.'

'That wouldn't have done any good.'

'Yes, it would. I wouldn't have let you do it.'

'You couldn't have stopped me. It was something between me and Riggins.'

'We could have just run away someplace.'

'No, we couldn't and you know it. You can't hide from a guy like him, not if he wants to find you. At least people like us can't. He had us both in a corner and he knew it. He was like an ornery little kid tearing wings off of a fly.

He'd have had me back in the pen on some trumped–up thing or another. And you'd have been sitting there like a trapped animal for the rest of your life. Or at least till he got tired of you and threw you out. You know that, don't you?'

She nodded her head.

'You think you're glad he's dead. I'm twice as glad as you are. I never did anything I felt better about. I hated his lousy guts. I couldn't stand the idea of you being in the same room with him, let alone in the same bed. I used to lay there at night and sweat, just from thinking about him. I never hurt anybody in my life on purpose. I never even kicked a dog. But I'd kill Riggins a dozen more times if I got the chance. I figure I'll get a nice Cadillac ride into heaven for what I done to him.'

'I know you were teasing me,' Thelma said then, 'about me working and saving money and buying stuff so we can live nice when you get out . . .'

'I wasn't teasing you.'

'Yes, you were. But it don't matter. That's what I was fixing to do anyway. That's what I want to do. When you get out we'll pretend that nothing bad ever happened. We'll just start over and live a decent life like regular people and have some fun together.'

They didn't talk about how long it would be. Thelma would be eligible for parole in three years but the judge had been very specific about Tucker. No consideration for parole until a minimum of twenty years had been served. Over a thousand weeks apart. More than seven thousand days. But they didn't talk about that.

CHAPTER TWENTY–SEVEN

JUST BEFORE HE left Applegate in the apartment in May-wood, Tucker said, 'It still doesn't make sense to me, Bob. How you'd go out of your way like you did, even hide out here away from your house like the police were looking for you, just so you wouldn't have to see me or talk to me.'

'Use your head, Roy. There's no mystery about it. As far as I knew you were a fugitive. That's what the papers said. That means if I know where you are I either have to tell the police or break the law myself. You know I could never turn you in to the police. I just couldn't do that. But I also couldn't put my neck on the block by helping you. I've got Corinne and the kids to think of. So I decided the less I knew about you the better. If I could avoid see-ing you or even talking to you I wouldn't know anything. I felt like a jackass, acting the way I have, but I didn't know any other way to handle it.'

Applegate watched from the window when Tucker went downstairs and left the building, got into his car and drove away. Across the street, two men were sitting in a mud–covered green sedan. They'd been sitting there for six hours but Applegate hadn't seen them till now.

The men watched Tucker pull away but they didn't fol-low him. After a few minutes one of them got out of the car, walked to the phone booth on the corner and made a call. Then he came back to the car.

Applegate stood watching from the window, his hands

suddenly damp and cold. He'd fooled Tucker but he couldn't fool himself – not any longer.

CHAPTER TWENTY–EIGHT

DRIVING EAST TOWARD Chicago, through the grimy desolation of the west side, Tucker felt a clutching pain in his insides, an ugly emptiness. He felt abandoned now in a new way. No jail or prison cell or army stockade had been like this. In a smoothly running car, money in his pocket, freedom to move and freedom to choose, he felt, for the first time in his life, permanently manacled and disarmed.

He'd staked everything on Applegate. All through the misery with Tagge and Pine and Reser, Brookshire and Henemyer, and Gaddis, all through the gut–wrenching jeopardy, the pain of deceiving Thelma, lying to her, seeing her confused and frightened, seeing her dead finally, crumpled by the road, all that time some stubborn internal voice had told him that Applegate would have answers for him, not solutions perhaps; but at least some information, some reasons for the crazy downhill plunge he'd been pushed into by a handful of quiet strangers in expensive suits.

Now he'd seen Applegate. He'd found him finally and forced his hand. He'd persisted and schemed and pushed through in a dogged way that was foreign to him, certain that he would come away with something he could use. Some information, some fact, some advice or guidance to follow, anything to give form or reason to the nightmare of blood and destruction he had witnessed since that day in the prison conference room when the warden, nervous and perspiring, had introduced him to a solid, grey–haired man who looked like a banker. The man had shaken his hand and said, 'I'm Marvin Tagge.'

But Applegate, the last hope, had stood in front of Tucker and slowly dissolved. Avoiding everything, rejecting everything, he had offered nothing, all in the name of self–preservation. 'You understand, Roy. I've got a lot at stake. I have to think of myself.'

Back in his hotel room, Tucker lay on his back on the bed, fully dressed, his hands behind his head, trying to plan something, trying to see some first step. The full–ahead conviction he'd shown to Applegate, that drive to have vengeance on Reser and Henemyer, lost steam now. Not through lack of hate or resolve, not because of fear for his own safety – none of that. Nothing he could see or imagine in some future month or year had any appeal or reality at all when measured beside the photo–sharp visions he had of Reser and Henemyer lying dead on the ground at his feet. It was the only life–purpose that made any sense to him: cushion Thelma's death somehow, soften the agonizing memories, by dumping two hated and lifeless bodies on the other pan of the scale. God, what pleasure that image gave him – quick fever, a rush of blood to his cheeks.

There was only one hurdle. He didn't know how to bring it off. He didn't know how to plan it, how to get into position, how to slip behind the lines, how to stand nose–to–nose, face–to–face at last, with Henemyer and Reser, and do it.

He had no lure now, no way to lead them to him. No threat and no weapon. He had seen the stories in the newspapers, the samples of handwriting exactly like his, read the word 'hoax' day after day. They had defused him. He knew that. The truth, his truth, had no explosive power now, no credibility. They had nothing to fear. They could ignore him, consider him as dead as the newspapers reported he was.

Tucker had been a hunter all his life. He had patience and stealth and cunning. Master of the still hunt, he had stood silent for hours waiting. Waiting as long as he had to for the possum, the raccoon, the snow rabbit, or the grey squirrel, blending with the background, the trees and country hedges, waiting for the game to show itself and die.

But there were days, he remembered many such days, when no stealth, no silence or patience, would work. The game simply did not, would not appear. The quarry stayed, warm and silent, in their burrows and nests or deep in the trunk of some tree.

Sometimes on those days they could be lured out. But usually not. Then the hunter, whatever his skill, went home empty-handed, no soft bodies in the game bag, no shots fired.

How could he lure Henemyer and Reser? How could he stalk them? Lying in his hotel room, feeling friendless and impotent, he could think of no way, find no way, see no solution.

CHAPTER TWENTY-NINE

AT MIDNIGHT THAT night, Corinne Applegate drove her husband's car from Oak Park to Maywood and parked it in front of the apartment building where Applegate was staying. She got out of the car and locked it as her children's governess, driving Corinne's station wagon, pulled up alongside. The governess slid across the front seat and Corinne got in behind the wheel, drove ahead to the corner and turned right.

Opposite the building entrance, the green sedan was gone now, replaced by a tan Chevrolet, one man in the driver's seat, another man in the back.

'Looks like the bird's about to fly,' the man in front said.

'I wouldn't be surprised.'

Applegate, wearing a mackinaw and a ski cap, stood at the window looking down at the tan car. The car stayed where it was, parked across the street at the curb.

Leaving all the lights on, Applegate turned away from the window, left the apartment by the kitchen service-door, and walked quickly along the corridor toward the back of the building. He ran down the rear stairs to the basement, walked through the furnace room and a long, dim–lit hall to the back door. He unlocked it, eased it open, and looked outside. Then he slipped out, closed the door behind him, climbed the outside basement stairs, and walked deliberately down the alley, his hands in his coat pockets.

When he came to the street he crossed it and walked two more blocks along another alley. Under the trees on a dark street Corinne's station wagon was parked, Corinne opposite the driver's seat, the motor running, the governess in the back seat.

Applegate got in behind the wheel, made a U–turn and headed north. No one spoke in the car. He drove five miles, then pulled in next to a cab stand at a busy intersection.

Corinne and the governess got out of the station wagon and into a taxi and Applegate drove straight ahead through the intersection, still heading north.

At Woodbridge Boulevard he turned east toward the lake. Where Woodbridge and Comiskey intersect, he pulled into a filling station, slid to a stop by the phone booth, and called Tucker.

'Are you asleep?'

'No. I was just sitting here.'

'I have to see you,' Applegate said.

'Where are you?'

'Listen closely. Don't drive your car. Take a cab to the Drake Hotel. Tell him to drop you at the north entrance. Walk straight through the lower lobby to the Walton Place entrance. Take another cab there and tell him to drive you to Wrigley Field. Just north of the main gate on Harrington there's an all–night coffee shop called Slayback's. Get out there, go inside, and have a cup of coffee at the counter. I'll be across the street in a brown station wagon. After ten minutes cross the street to where I'm parked. If I'm not there that means I saw somebody tailing you. If that happens I'll be gone. You can go back to your hotel and go to sleep.'

It was almost forty minutes later when Tucker walked out of Slayback's, crossed Harrington Avenue and got into the car with Applegate.

'You think I'm crazy?' Applegate said.

'I don't know what's going on.'

'I've been holding out on you. That's the main thing that's going on.'

CHAPTER THIRTY

'Jesus . . . I don't believe my ears,' Tucker said. He was sitting in a booth with Applegate in an after–hours tavern west of Skokie. 'You're the last guy in the world . . .'

'It's not the way it sounds,' Applegate said. 'I steered Tagge to you but only because he lied to me. I didn't have

103

any idea what they were up to. I thought I was doing you a favour. But as soon as you were out of prison, when I saw those stories that said you'd killed your cellmate, I knew I'd been had. By then it was too late.'

'Tagge and you. How did you know Tagge?'

'I'd known him for twenty years – almost that. He tried to recruit me for an intelligence job when I was still in Princeton. I turned him down but he wouldn't accept it. Kept after me hot and heavy for six months. We got to be friends and we stayed friends from then on.'

'What do you mean, an intelligence job?'

'Just that. It was a big thing then in the eastern schools. Maybe it still is. Some of the brightest guys in my class ended up in one of the intelligence agencies – Central, Treasury, Secret Service. It was the same at Yale and Harvard. They went for the best and the brightest. There was a real mystique about it, a chance to be on the *inside* inside, know a lot of secrets. The recruiters were all smooth apples. Three–hundred–dollar suits and an answer for everything. Or if you were a jock they sent a jock recruiter after you. Anyway, a lot of guys I knew went for it. And I was intrigued myself. But I had this thing about medical school. So I wasn't about to walk away from that.'

'Why are you telling me this now? Why didn't you tell me before? Why not this afternoon when I saw you?'

'I thought I could play dumb. Once I found out Whittaker was dead and when it came out that you were connected with it, I knew I was in trouble. There had to be a blood bath. Dallas all over again. Anybody who could connect all the links had to go. That's why they killed Tagge and Thelma and that's why they'll kill you. And me too.'

'I thought you said . . .'

'I know what I said. I thought I still had a chance to squeeze by. But now that I've seen you . . .'

'They don't know that.'

'The hell they don't. And now they'll assume that I know everything *you* know. All the names and places. And they're right. I do.'

'But how do they . . .'

'When you left my place today, two guys were watching you from a car across the street. At least I thought they were watching you. Only they didn't leave when you did. They stayed there – watching me. And when they left, some new guys took their place.'

'That means it's my fault.'

'No, it's not. It's nobody's fault except mine. If I hadn't put Tagge onto you . . .'

'I still don't know why you did that, Bob. How did it happen.'

'I told you, Tagge and I were friends. After I left Princeton he used to come to Boston to see Corinne and me when I was in medical school. He'd drop in every few months. And later when I was interning in Fort Worth we saw him there. And we wrote to each other when I was in Vietnam and Japan. I mean I thought of him as a very close friend. Like an uncle, only better. Matter of fact he's the godfather to my oldest daughter. I would have trusted him with everything, any secret, any information.'

'But you said he lied to you.'

'He sure did. I was a sitting duck. He'd really set me up. He'd always been very open with me, discussed things he was doing, hush–hush things, when we were by ourselves. There was never any doubt that he trusted me. So I trusted him. He used to say, "I know I never managed to recruit you but I pretend to myself I did." So that's the way it was. He treated me like a kind of junior officer, somebody he was training and confiding in. He always left out the names and the dates and the places, almost always, but he told me some hair–raising stuff.'

After Applegate dropped him off at the north shore terminal in Evanston, after he rode back to the near north side and walked from the station to his hotel, Tucker sat in his room with the lights on, Applegate's words playing back in his brain like a recording.

'Tagge had told me before about a man named Rolf Zimmer. He was a former party official who had defected from East Germany and he was important for two reasons: one,

105

for what he could tell our intelligence people, and two, for what the East Germans thought he could tell. He was a trump card, a black ace. The only catch was he died suddenly about six weeks after he came over. But the Soviet people in this country didn't know he was dead so they kept worrying about him. And Tagge and his friends wanted them to keep worrying. They wanted the world to believe that Zimmer was still alive and available as an information source. So they needed a proxy, an anonymous man they could move around from one safe house to another. Nobody would get a good look at him but he would be, as far as anybody knew, Rolf Zimmer. According to Tagge, most of our intelligence people had never seen Zimmer and didn't know he was dead. So they would be fooled too.

'Tagge said it would be a short–term thing. Six months to a year. By then they would have exhausted whatever psychological value Zimmer had. Then the man who had impersonated him would be given a new identity and a government income for life.

'When he told me all this I said the problem was to find somebody who would be willing to give up his own identity and change his whole life. Tagge said, "We'll get somebody who doesn't have a life. We're going to take a man out of prison."

'I thought about what he'd said. I thought about it a lot. And the next time I saw him I told him about you. I admit I had some doubts about it. It sounded like a strange manoeuvre. But I trusted Tagge. And I figured even if there was some risk involved it might be worth it to you. Better than spending half your life in jail.'

'Why didn't he tell me he knew you?' Tucker said.

'I asked him not to. I wanted you to listen to what he had to say and make up your own mind. I didn't want you to be influenced by me.'

'Jesus . . . now it starts to make sense. I never could figure how they picked me. The prisons are full of guys but they zeroed in on me. Now I see why.'

'It wasn't just on my say–so. I'm sure they checked out

everything they could about you – military record, family, the whole works.'

Tucker nodded. 'Tagge knew every move I'd ever made.'

'Anyway, now you know. I thought I was doing you a favour but it didn't turn out that way. Now we're both running.'

'What would happen if you went to the police?'

'I've thought of that. But what would I tell them? Nobody has done anything to me. I haven't been threatened. I can't give them any real evidence of anything.'

'What if we both went?'

'It wouldn't solve anything, Roy. If it would, you'd have done it a long time ago. They had the Hobart warden in their pocket and you can bet your ass, when the chips are down, they've got the local police in their pocket. This is big stuff, Washington DC, a federal case. I guarantee you that all roads lead back to your friend Reser. If we went to the police, we'd end up sitting in a locked room with that bastard.'

'I'd like that. That's what I want.'

'Not by his rules you don't. You'd be dog meat in twenty minutes.' Applegate lit a cigarette and squinted through the smoke at Tucker. 'I'm telling you, Roy. There's only one thing for you to do. Disappear. That's what I'm going to do.'

'What about your wife and kids?'

'That's the main reason I'm doing it. There's no danger to them if I'm not around.'

After they left the tavern, while they drove to the north–shore station, Applegate said, 'The missing piece in all this, the part that nobody can figure out, is why anybody would want to kill Whittaker.'

'I know the answer to that.' Tucker told Applegate the story that Henemyer had told him – about Whittaker's involvement with the Chinese.

'He's nuts.'

'Maybe he is but that's what he told me.'

107

'I have never heard such bullshit in my life. You notice they haven't tried to leak that story. They know better. Because nobody in his right mind would believe it. Whittaker was as rich as Rockefeller, for Christ's sake. The Army was just an activity for him. So was politics. He didn't need a dime from the South Vietnamese or anybody else. And he was so bloody conservative he wouldn't stay in the same hotel with a Communist, let alone pass along government secrets. The South Vietnamese may have been kicking back to somebody but it's a cinch it wasn't Whittaker.'

When Applegate pulled in at the curb by the train station, he said, 'The truth is, I'd bet my life on it, that Reser and his friends are up to something rotten and Whittaker was about to blow the whistle on them. And I wouldn't be surprised if I know what it is.'

'What do you mean?'

'I haven't got all the pieces together yet. Tagge told me all kinds of stories about Reser, most of them are so far–fetched that even Tagge couldn't believe them. He thought Reser was crazy as a bedbug.'

'Then why did he work with him?'

'Good question. Politics makes strange bedfellows, I guess.'

Just before Tucker got out of the car, Applegate said, 'Remember that garrison bag you brought back from Japan with your war souvenirs and pictures of all your Geisha girl–friends. I've been keeping it for you. You want it?'

'I don't think so.'

'I've got it stashed in my garage up in the country. No problem to send it if you want it.'

Tucker shook his head. 'No thanks, Bob.'

'Suit yourself.' Then, 'I think I'll send it anyway. If you don't want it, you can throw it out.'

As soon as Tucker got out of the car and started up the outside steps to the train platform, Applegate pulled away from the curb and headed west on Dempster. In the rear view mirror he saw a car following him. When he turned

north on the Tri-state Tollway, the car was still there –
obviously, openly, a hundred yards behind him. It stayed
with him all the way into Wisconsin.

CHAPTER THIRTY–ONE

Two DAYS LATER Tucker had a note from Applegate, a
small key enclosed with the note, and a clipping.

> Here is the key to your garrison bag. I'm keeping one in
> case you lose this one. I'll ship you the bag in a couple of
> days. Also here's a clipping I cut out of a magazine a few
> months ago. I think it will interest you. It sure as hell inter-
> ests me. Things are starting to come together in my head.
> When I solve the puzzle, if I do, I'll let you know.
>
> > Best always,
> > *Bob*

Tucker unfolded the clipped–out article and read it carefully.

When the President of the United States and his Vice-
President are charter members of a little–known organisation whose total membership includes the major bankers
and industrialists in the United States, Japan and West
Germany, as well as the rulers of Saudia Arabia and Iran,
does that mean something?

When we learn that the President, a minor political figure and modestly successful businessman before his election, was affiliated with this odd organisation three years before he became a candidate for President, when we learn that this group is openly committed to influencing presidential elections, although they claim no connection with any political party, should that make us wonder?

Questions proliferate. Is all that wealth and power serving the best interests of the people? Is the democratic process still what it was intended to be? Is it mere coincidence that the President, his Vice-President, the Secretary of State, the National Security Chief, and eighteen other top presidential appointees are all members of this small and élite international group?

The mind begins to dance. What are the ramifications? What are the objectives? The group, which calls itself Interworld Alliance, admits that it aspires to a position of high–level international influence, something apolitical, *extra*–political, a kind of world government outside government that speaks the language of business. Profit and loss, expansion and growth, acquisition, manipulation, and planned obsolescence. Brave New World, Man and Superman, business is business, money talks.

Frightening? We think so. How can a creed that ignores national boundaries, that by-passes elected governments and their officials, have any regard at all for one solitary and unimportant individual, whatever his colour, religion or national origin? It can't, of course. By its own definition of itself.

There is a rationale and it is this: strong international links, in economics and business and banking, are deterrents to armed conflict. In short, Greed discourages War. History, we believe, tells us otherwise. But assuming for the moment that such a theory is true, why would the charter membership of Interworld Alliance include three retired generals, two retired admirals, and one former Chief of the Central Intelligence Agency? And why particularly a man like Thomas Reser?

Reser retired early from the military because his abrasive speeches were too much even for the Pentagon. Our Government advocates *détente* with the Soviet Union. Reser is a tireless Red-baiter. As an active general, he pressed for an invasion of China through North Korea. At the time of the Cuban missile crisis he recommended saturation-bombing of Cuba. In a country that has consistently defended and supported the position of Israel, Reser is privately anti–Semitic and publicly pro–Arab. He is a frequent and welcome guest in the palaces and sheikdoms of the oil–producing countries. They speak of him as a friend, a supporter, a strong ally.

In an organisation of bankers and industrialists what is the value of such a man? What role does he play as confidential advisor to the President of the United States? No answers come from the Oval Office. More surprising, no one is even asking the questions.

One thought nags and persists. Perhaps we are beginning at last to see what President Whittaker meant, in his final speech before leaving office, when he said, 'Our greatest future danger, the thing we have most to fear, is the growing power of the industrial and military complex.'

CHAPTER THIRTY–TWO

A LIGHT SNOW was falling in Southern Wisconsin. It had begun at noon. Now there was a thin accumulation on the ground outside Applegate's house, turning the driveway silver, glistening in the cold sunshine on the shrubs and trees and on the lawn that sloped down to the edge of the lake.

All that morning Applegate had tried to write a letter to Corinne. After breakfast he'd sat for three hours at the typewriter desk in the den. Several times he finished one

111

paragraph. Once he typed half a page. But it wasn't going well. He wanted to tell her the truth but he couldn't. He hated lying to her but he had to. Trying to stay as close to the facts as he could, trying at the same time not to frighten her, he foundered. Over and over.

Finally he gave up, put on a heavy sweater and a wool cap, went out behind the house to the woodpile and began to chop kindling for the fireplace.

He worked hard for more than an hour. Then he made several trips to the wood–box on the back porch. After he'd filled it, he stacked the rest of the wood he'd cut on the floor by the stone fireplace in the living room.

Taking off his sweaty clothes, he shaved, showered, and got dressed again. He went down to the kitchen, made a Braunschweiger-and-cheese sandwich, and washed it down with a bottle of beer. Then he went back into the den, sat down at the typewriter and wrote the letter to Corinne.

Dear Corinne,

I'm here. I'm settled in and everything's fine. I got in a lot of food and everything is working smoothly in the house. I'm warm and cozy.

I've been thinking about you a lot. I hated just dropping you off at a taxi-stand and driving away like that. I know you're worried sick and that makes me feel lousy. I wish I could put my arms around you and say, 'It's all right. Everything's going to be fine.' But I can't do that. Not yet.

Everything is going to be fine. I'm sure of it. You know me. I don't think there's any problem that can't be solved.

I can hear you saying to yourself, 'What problem? What is it? Why can't he tell me?'

I will tell you. As soon as I can. I never keep secrets from you. I'm no good at it. But for now, till a few more things get clarified, you'll just have to sit tight. Some things I can say now. If you're worried that I've done something wrong or dishonest or illegal – I haven't. It's just that an odd situation exists and I'm involved in it in an accidental way. Because of other people. And I don't mean Roy. He's involved in it, too, but he's not the cause of it. I mean I'm not stuck up here in the woods because of Roy Tucker. So don't blame him. You see why I can't explain anything? The more I say the cloudier it gets.

Here's the news you're not going to like. I don't want you to bring the girls up here for the holidays. I know they'll be disappointed but there's nothing to be done. I won't be here. By the time you get this letter, I'll be gone. But as soon as I get to where I'm going, I'll let you know where I am.

I know you'll be frantic when you read this letter but there's no way I can prevent that. You just have to trust me. I've got good sense, remember that, and I'm doing the best I can for us under the circumstances. Kiss the kids for me and if anybody asks, stick with your story. As far as you know, I'm still in San Francisco or Seattle or on an airplane someplace.

I love you, Sport. See you soon.
Bob

After he addressed and stamped the envelope to Corinne, he took a small tape recorder out of the bottom desk drawer, snapped a fresh cassette into position, pressed the *record* button, and tested the tape. He talked into it, said five or six words, then ran it back and listened. He erased the test words then, rewound to the edge, pressed *record* again, and began to talk quietly into the concealed microphone.

Late that afternoon he drove down to Janesville, mailed Corinne's letter, and shipped a cardboard carton to Tucker, his canvas garrison bag stuffed inside. All the way to Janesville and back it seemed that no one was following him. But when he was half a mile from home, he saw the car he'd seen before, parked on a side road, the engine running, the wipers brushing the light, feathery snow off the windshield.

CHAPTER THIRTY–THREE

'TAGGE IS A perfect case in point,' Reser said. 'Marvin Tagge is a perfect example of what I'm talking about.' He and Henemyer were sitting in the back seat of a chauffeured government limousine, speeding south on the Capitol Beltway, heading for Andrews Air Base.

'Don't get me wrong,' he went on. 'Marvin was a gifted man. Nobody ever had better natural gifts for intelligence work. He was smart and patient and tough–minded. He wasn't afraid of anything and he had a good nose for a situation. He could smell out a lie like a bloodhound. The fact that he wasn't a soldier didn't seem to hamper him. Marvin never served one day in the military. As far as I know he never fired a weapon. But he had an instinct for tactics and position and deployment. He always knew where everybody was at any given moment.

'A great eye for detail, too. And a first–rate memory. Like I say, all the ingredients. But that other thing, what we were talking about before, he didn't have that at all. He couldn't cut off, couldn't isolate and say, "That's the target. That's what must be done."

'Marvin's problem was he thought everything was connected, one way or the other. He thought if you made a mistake you had to live with it. What he couldn't do was just act. He was always looking for the best solution and sometimes there's no time for that. Sometimes, lots of times, you have to shoot from the hip and pick up the pieces later. Or just let the pieces lay there and rot. When the game was dirty poker with somebody else's cards, Marvin kept trying to play bridge.

'That's what screwed us with Tucker. Tagge couldn't accept the fact that we'd found ourselves a shooter, a mechanic, nothing more. When we burned that helicopter, Tucker should have been in it – end of the road. Instead of that, we've still got him floating around. And now we've got Applegate, too, another one of Tagge's leftovers. He couldn't play it smart. He had to line up with Tucker.'

'It's all right, Tom. Applegate is making it easy for us. And Tucker can dangle forever now.'

'I don't think so.'

'At least he can dangle till you get back from the Middle East on December 22nd.'

'23rd.'

'23rd,' Henemyer said. 'After that, if he's still making you nervous we'll relocate him. By the first of the year, the party will be over.'

Reser grinned behind his cigar. 'At the first of the year, the party starts.'

Forty minutes later an Air Force jet took off from Andrews, Henemyer alone in the passenger section, leafing through a magazine and sipping Cutty Sark.

The plane banked sharply, climbing at a sharp angle, and headed west toward Wisconsin. Two hours later it set down smoothly on the private landing strip of an electronics plant just outside Beloit.

A car was waiting for Henemyer. He drove north on Highway 90, then angled off on State Road 26 toward Lake Koshkonong.

CHAPTER THIRTY–FOUR

APPLEGATE LISTENED TO the six o'clock evening news on the Madison radio station while he cooked himself some ham and eggs and fried potatoes and ate them at the kitchen table. Instead of coffee, he drank a glass of milk. He didn't want to risk lying awake.

When he finished eating he made four thick sandwiches, ham and cheese on rye bread, wrapped each one neatly in aluminium foil, and put them in his rucksack on top of the two shirts and fresh socks and underwear he'd already folded and packed away there.

After he washed the dishes and the skillet, after he'd wiped off the drainboard and put everything away, he went upstairs, undressed and got into bed. It was seven–fifteen. He had left the downstairs lights on in the living room and den just like any other night. And a fire burning in the fireplace.

He slept till ten–thirty when the alarm went off. He got up, turned off the downstairs lights, banked the fire, reset the alarm clock for two–thirty in the morning, and went back to bed.

This time he didn't sleep well. His head was filled with routes and roads, checkpoints and timetables. Finally, around midnight, he managed to fall asleep. When the alarm went off again he was sleeping soundly.

He got up and dressed in the dark. Thermal underwear, boot socks over light wool socks, corduroy pants tucked into his snow boots, a woollen shirt, a heavy sweater, and a hip–length, down–filled parka with game pockets in the back.

Before he slipped the rucksack on his shoulders, he walked through the ground–floor rooms of the house, stood at the windows in the darkness and stared out, looking for movement, for the flicker of a match, studied the half–cleared terrain on all sides of the house.

Just before he left the house he checked the fireplace, stirred the dead ashes carefully to make sure there were no half–burned butts of logs hidden there. Then he walked quickly to the back door, let himself out, and closed the door softly behind him.

He stood frozen against the back wall of the house, out of sight in the shadows, watching, listening. Like a camouflage screen on demand, a soft heavy snow began to float down.

At last he stepped away from the house and walked across thirty yards of open space to the edge of the woods. Twenty feet in, he stopped again, invisible against the trunk of a thick tree, and stood there, barely breathing, watching and listening, for long minutes. Then he moved ahead through the veil of snow, through the heavy winter woods.

He knew this land like he knew his pocket. He had tramped and trailed and explored it, back and forth, in all seasons, for twenty miles around. No one could lose him here, not even now, in the snow, in the black night of winter.

He sensed landmarks that he couldn't see. His feet remembered even when his eyes didn't. Still, unwilling to risk anything, he had chosen the simplest foolproof routes. Around the north edge of the lake, keeping it close always, just to his right, moving steadily east till the Rock River stopped him, just where it emptied into Lake Kosh-konong, then along the north river bank into Fort Atkin-son, an eight–mile hike, nine at the most.

He would catch the six–thirty Greyhound at the high-way terminal just outside Fort Atkinson, change at

Madison for the Canadian Express, be in Duluth by mid–afternoon and in Thunder Bay, Ontario, by supper time.

The woods were soft and spectral, moon–white, without life, it seemed, without birds or animals, quilted, floored with cotton wool, ceilinged with black velvet. And the silence could be felt almost, tasted, like snowflakes on the tongue. There was depth to it, and dimension. It was so total that it challenged the ears. Applegate strained to hear something, anything, other than his own cushioned footfalls in the new snow.

Two or three times, when he imagined he'd heard a twig snap, or a low branch, disturbed, swing back into place, he stopped moving. The silence, however, when he froze to listen, was pristine and unchanged. The whiteness and the stillness lulled him, enfolded him as he moved north and east around the lake toward the bank of the black river that would lead him into Fort Atkinson.

He didn't see Henemyer. Never saw his face. And didn't hear him until he spoke. Suddenly the bright glare of a flashlight beam shone in his eyes, stopping him, blinding him. Then the voice, 'Don't panic, Dr Applegate. Don't even move. That's good. Very good. Now I want you to turn around and walk to that first tree just behind you. Put your arms around it and press your forehead up against the bark. That's good. That's fine. That's perfect.'

Applegate sensed someone moving in close behind him. Then everything stopped.

CHAPTER THIRTY–FIVE

IT WAS TEN–FIFTEEN in the morning when the Wisconsin State Police called Corinne Applegate. An hour later, she and her brother, Jack Easter, were on the tollway heading north, Jack driving, Corinne pale and silent beside him.

When they drove into Janesville, Jack said, 'Where do we go?'

'The police station. In the courthouse, they said. On the town square.'

Francis Digby, the Police Chief of Janesville, was waiting for them in his office. And Captain Wayne Leeks of the State Police. Leeks took Corinne to the county morgue to identify Applegate's body. Then they came back to Digby's office.

'We won't keep you any longer than necessary. But there are certain details we have to go over.' Digby opened a file folder on his desk. 'Dr Applegate's body was discovered at about six o'clock this morning, on the north bank of Lake Koshkonong, approximately seven miles southwest of Fort Atkinson. Our coroner, Dr Echols, estimates the time of death as four–thirty in the morning. Cause of death – drowning. When the body was discovered it was lying face down at the edge of the lake. The head and shoulders were in the water.'

There was an empty silence. Jack Easter looked at his sister. She was looking down at the floor.

'How far was he from his house?' Jack said.

This time Captain Leeks answered. 'A little over two miles. Between two and three.'

'It doesn't make sense. Why would he be walking around the woods in the middle of the night?'

'Sometimes hunters like to get an early start. Even the ice fishermen . . .'

'Bob wasn't a hunter,' Corinne said. 'He never shot an animal in his life.'

'He didn't have a rifle with him, did he?' Jack said.

Digby looked at Leeks. Leeks shook his head. 'We didn't find a rifle, but that doesn't mean . . .'

'Bob didn't even own a rifle,' Corinne said.

'Who found him?' Jack said.

'Two boys named Pritchett. They live on the farm that adjoins the Applegate land on the west. They pulled the body up out of the water. Then one of them ran home and told his father and he called the State Police.'

'It doesn't make sense,' Corinne said.

'Your husband had a rucksack on his back. There were a few sandwiches in it and some clean clothes. Shirts and socks and underwear. It looked as if he planned to be away for a little while. Was he a hiker? Was he likely to go off by himself?'

'Are you trying to say . . .'

'We're not trying to say anything, Mr Easter,' Digby said. 'We know this is a difficult time for you and your sister. We're simply trying to give you all the information we have. There's no question about the cause of death. It was drowning. And there's no evidence to indicate it was anything but a freak accident.'

'Does it make sense to you?' Jack said.

'Accidents never make sense,' Leeks said.

'You don't feel as if there are some pieces missing?'

'You bet we do,' Digby said. 'We don't know why he was out there in the woods in the middle of the night. We don't know why he was carrying food and extra clothes. And we don't know why he ended up face down in the water. Did he pass out? Did he trip and fall and hit his head? We don't know.'

'We're faced with four possibilities in any unexplained death. Natural causes, an accident, suicide, or homicide. The only one we can rule out in this case is natural causes.'

'Are you implying that he killed himself?' Corinne said.

'No. I don't think your husband killed himself. But I can't guarantee it. I don't think it was homicide either but I can't guarantee it wasn't. I can guarantee you that we'll find whatever evidence there is. We have three detective teams on the case and they'll stay on it till every possibility has been checked out. We know already that there was no evidence of any disturbance in the house. There were no bruises or contusions on the body and no signs of any struggle on the river bank. So unless you tell us that Dr Applegate had been threatened, unless you know of someone who would have profited from his death, we have to conclude, from what we've seen so far, that the cause of death was drowning, and that it was an accident.'

'Did your husband have any enemies that you're aware of?'

Of all the answers she might have given, Corinne selected one without hesitation. 'No,' she said. And as she heard her own voice sounding small and strange and secretive, she realized that now she would never know any of the things she was burning to know. Whatever secrets Bob had carried with him were still with him. No amount of soil–sifting or chemical analysis or interrogation would ever bring them out. And even if she knew, what good would it do her? Dimly she heard Jack and Captain Leeks discussing the possibility of an autopsy.

'No. I don't want that,' she said. 'I can't stand the thought of all that. I'm sure you're right. I'm sure it was some kind of senseless accident that none of us will ever understand.'

Corinne's instinct was correct. If an autopsy had taken place it would have provided additional questions but no answers. She would have learned only that Applegate was peacefully tranquillized when he died, that he had no pain as he lay in the lake shallows, the water slowly filling his lungs. She would have had no clue as to who had placed him there or why.

CHAPTER THIRTY–SIX

THE DAY AFTER Applegate's death, Tucker stopped at the lobby desk on his way out to breakfast and told the clerk he'd be checking out at noon.

'I'll have your bill ready, Mr Brookshire.' As Tucker turned away, the clerk said, 'There's an envelope here for you.'

Tucker came back to the desk. 'When did that come in?'

'Somebody must have dropped it off when the night man was here. I just noticed it when I put your key in the box.'

Roy took the plain envelope and tore it open. There was a clipping inside from the Beloit evening paper, yesterday's edition. The headline read: OAK PARK DOCTOR DROWNING VICTIM.

Tucker stood in the centre of the lobby reading the item. One column. Twenty–seven lines. He read it quickly. Then again slowly. He crumpled it in his hand, walked out onto the street and dropped it in the gutter.

Turning west he walked to the corner, turned south on Dearborn and fought the cold wind for nearly three blocks before he found an open tavern. Inside, in the warm dark, he climbed up on a bar stool and ordered a drink.

The clock on the back wall said ten o'clock. Half a dozen

silent morning drinkers were already there, scattered along the bar, fully involved, making no overtures and welcoming none. No conversation. No eye contact. A sign over the cash register, screwed to the back bar mirror, capsulised the atmosphere: *Drinking is a serious business. Don't bother me.*

Sixteen hours later, when the bar closed, Tucker was still on the same bar stool. Sitting mute and immobile, no dizziness or blurred vision, able to gesture when his glass was empty, able to make it down the length of the bar to the toilet and return, but paralysed in some very real and clinical sense from the inside out, he did not drool or vomit, stagger and fall, or wet himself. Managing somehow to avoid the symptoms of drunkenness, he was nonetheless dead drunk, numbed and desensitised, all feelings cut off except the sensory and rudimentary motor necessities. Walk, breathe, urinate, lift the glass, swallow. Beyond that, nothing needed or permitted. No think, no feel, no function.

It was twelve degrees below zero when he began the slow, past–two–in–the–morning return to the Bridgman. He stayed close to the buildings when his legs could manage it, the right elbow angled out like an antenna – a guide, a feeler, a support when needed. His face down inside his turned–up collar, hands deep in his overcoat pockets, he stumbled ahead, lurching and slipping but staying miraculously upright till he spun himself through the revolving door at last into the over–warm lobby of the Bridgman.

When he woke up the next day at noon, the pain in his head occupied him totally, the after effects accomplishing beautifully what the alcohol had done before.

He got up, gathered yesterday's clothes from the floor around the bed, and put them on. Twenty minutes later he was in the same bar again, on the same stool, his overcoat on the wall hook beside him, the bartender coolly accustomed, it seemed, to red and ruined eyes, death–grey skin, foul bourbon breath, and stubbly chins.

'What'll it be?' he said.

'Old Crow. A double. Water on the side and four aspirin tablets.'

The second day went as smoothly as the first. The numbness took over again and intensified. The dead men stayed away. And the women. Even Thelma. She remained in her hillside grave in Costa Rica, made no effort to take a stool in any bar whatsoever on Dearborn Street in Chicago. Spiventa didn't buck and twitch as the bullets ripped through him on the dunes north of Hobart; Whittaker's face didn't explode in the sunshine as it had in memory a thousand times since that first time; Tagge's car, with him inside, didn't blast apart in a red–orange flame; Brookshire and Pine didn't tangle together spurting blood, at the foot of the stairs outside the house near Puntarenas. And Applegate stayed firmly alive – bright and capable, able to understand and adjust and survive.

As a small death, bloodless and self–willed, the alcohol escape worked well for Tucker, worked through the second day just as it had through the first. But this time it worked too well. At seven–thirty in the evening, his eyes rolled back in his head suddenly, his mouth sagged open, and he pitched, dead–weight, straight back, the stool falling with him, to the floor.

When he found the hotel key in Tucker's overcoat pocket, the bartender, instead of calling the police, called the Bridgman. An hour later Tucker was in his hotel room, in his bed. This time the bellman hung up his clothes.

At six the next morning, Tucker woke up. He called for a double order of toast, some bacon and a pot of black coffee. After he ate and drank the coffee, he felt better. After he shaved and sat in the bathtub for an hour, drank several glasses of water, and put on clean clothes, he felt better still. He called the desk and said, 'I need the morning paper. And the papers for the last two days. Can you manage that?'

When the papers came he checked all the obituary columns. In the oldest paper, the one from two days before, he found Applegate's funeral notice. At first Tucker thought it was over, then he double–checked the date. The funeral would be later that morning. At eleven o'clock. In the First Presbyterian Church, corner of Wyandotte and Dautel in Oak Park.

Afraid of being late and conspicuous, Tucker was conspicuously early. He parked across the street, down the block from the church entrance, and waited, watching the people arrive.

He saw Corinne enter the church with her two daughters. And hundreds of other people. Gleaming cars. Fine clothes and furs. White–faced, stunned and serious people bundled up against the cold, hurrying from their cars to the church, then having to wait shivering on the steps as the crowd filled the doorway.

Tucker had planned to slip in at the last and sit in the back, be the last one in after everyone was seated. But when two young men in black suits pulled the heavy doors shut and disappeared inside, he made no move to get out of his car.

He stayed there with the motor idling and the heater on as the bells began to toll at the top of the tower, sat turned in his seat facing the church entrance for a long quiet time, almost an hour, till the bells began to toll again, slow and heavy, till the doors swung open, and the people came out, moving more quickly now, hurrying to their cars.

The hearse came around from the rear of the church, turned the corner and moved slowly along the street past Tucker's car. Then the long procession of cars, Corinne and the children in the first one just behind the hearse, the others following in a tight column.

As the last cars passed, the cars parked near the church pulled out from the curb and joined the line. And when the very last car had rolled by, Tucker pulled out, caught up with it, and followed along, bringing up the rear, police holding traffic at all the intersections so the funeral cars could pass without stopping.

At the cemetery, the long procession crept slowly through the stone gateway, then fanned out from its rigid single line as cars angled off on connecting driveways through the pattern of trees and monuments and hurried ahead to park as close as possible to the open grave on a frozen ground–rise at the west end of the cemetery.

Tucker parked on a residential street outside the gates and walked in, up the main driveway, following behind the ragged lines of people leaving their cars and walking by twos and threes across the hard ground, up the incline toward the grave site. The old people stayed behind in the cars, bundled in lap robes, staying warm, watching the activity on the hill through frosted windows.

People were ten or fifteen deep around the grave. Tucker didn't try to get close. He stopped downslope from the crowd, stood with his back against a wide–branching walnut tree. He could see the bright–coloured top edge of a high bank of floral pieces and he could hear the thin voice of the minister cutting through, saying final prayers, but he couldn't see anything that was taking place at the grave edge. Only when the people backed away, turned away, and moved in all directions to their cars, did he realise that the ceremony, the praying and the coffin–lowering, were over.

Tucker stood where he was as people streamed past him, noses red, breath clouding in the cold air. When everyone except a grey–haired funeral attendant and three graveyard workers had left the grave, Tucker walked up the rise, stopped at the lip of the dug–out grave, and looked down at the top of the vault, a blanket of red roses spread across it.

It was nothing to him. Just an ugly hole in the frozen ground. A box with a body in it. He couldn't connect it with Applegate. He remembered looking down at his mother's coffin when he was twelve years old. 'That's not her. There's nothing there. I can't cry over a strange casket. I'll cry later when I miss the way she was. When I want to hear her or smell her or touch her, that's when I'll cry. For what's *missing*. I can't cry now just looking at what's left.'

When he turned away from the grave, most of the cars had already left or were pulling away. But the hearse was still there. And the black limousine behind it, the one Corinne and her children were riding in.

It never occurred to Tucker to speak to her. He angled

away from her car and headed across the grass, between the monuments and headstones, toward the gate. He was half–way there when she caught up with him.

'Roy . . . my God . . . I almost didn't know you. Are you all right?' He was hatless and pale, his eyes red and wounded, his cheeks hollow and sunken. 'Are you sick? You look . . .'

'No. I'm all right.'

'Were you at the church?'

'I didn't come in. I waited outside.'

'I didn't realise . . . I mean I didn't know you were still in Chicago.'

'I'm leaving this afternoon.'

'I feel so rotten,' she said then. 'There's so much I don't understand. Couldn't we talk a little? Couldn't you come back to the house and have some coffee?'

He stood looking at her, didn't answer, and she began to cry. 'It's all crazy. They said Bob went walking in the woods in the middle of the night. They said he drowned accidentally in the lake. It's just so senseless and crazy . . . it's got me crazy. They even said maybe he drowned himself. *You* knew Bob. He wouldn't . . . he could never . . .'

There was a long silence. Over her shoulder, Tucker could see three men from the funeral home standing beside the hearse watching them. A little girl leaned out of the limousine window and called, 'Mommy!'

'I have to go, Corinne, ' Tucker said.

'Can you come back to the house? It would mean a lot to me to be able to talk to you. I need . . .'

'I can't.'

'Please. There are things about Bob . . . I mean it's terrible when you think you know everything about someone, then you find out there are all kinds of secrets.'

'I don't know anything. I don't know any secrets.'

'Just tell me one thing. Did you see him before he went up to Wisconsin?'

'Yes.'

'Then you know things I don't know.'

'I don't know anything, Corinne.'

127

'You mean you won't tell.'

'I mean I don't know.'

She pulled her coat close around her. Her face was pale and pinched suddenly. 'You're a liar, Roy.'

'You think what you want to.'

'I should have known I couldn't expect anything from you. You're trouble and you always have been. And you're bad luck. You brought Bob nothing but bad luck.'

'He was the best friend I ever had, Corinne.'

'I knew it the first time he wrote me about you. I knew it when he brought you home from Vietnam. Bob thought he could turn you into something you're not. But I never believed it.'

'I know you didn't. I didn't believe it either. That's why I left when I did.'

They stood silent, facing each other. The wind had died down. It felt warmer suddenly. Soft snowflakes began to fall, sticking to his hair, to her fur hat, and the shoulders of their coats.

Finally she said, 'If Bob had never met you, he wouldn't be dead now. I don't know how I know that but I know it.'

She turned away and walked back to the limousine. Roy stood watching her through the fine screen of snow till she got in and the door closed behind her. Then he walked out to the street, got into his car, and drove back to his hotel in Chicago.

PART THREE

CHAPTER THIRTY–SEVEN

AFTER TUCKER PAID his bill and checked out of the Bridgman, as he walked to the parking lot, heavy snow falling, two or three inches already on the ground, the bellman, carrying a bulky cardboard carton tied with twine, caught up with him. 'This box is for you. They delivered it this morning.'

Tucker knew when he saw Applegate's name and Wisconsin address in the upper left hand corner of the address sticker that it was the garrison bag, the war relic, souvenir of another time and another life.

He was tempted to leave it behind, to tell the hotel man to throw it out, but when he opened the car trunk to put in his suitcase, he said, 'Just toss it in there. Thanks a lot.'

As he moved south on the tollway out of the sprawl of Chicago, blizzard warnings buzzed on the car radio. Between South Chicago and Danville, Illinois, he could drive no faster than thirty miles an hour, sometimes as slow as twenty. Or ten. It was nine o'clock at night before he reached Terre Haute, Indiana, only a hundred and fifty miles south of Chicago.

The wind had come up by then and the snow was driving and swirling, drifting shoulder high along the road. At midnight when he rolled slowly through Vincennes heading south toward Evansville, the state troopers stopped him at the roadblock. The highway was closed.

He stayed in a motel at the edge of Vincennes till noon

of the following day. By then the temperature had dropped to twenty below zero, the wind had died down, and the snow had stopped.

The roads to the north were drifted and clogged, abandoned cars and overturned trucks, but south of Vincennes, where the total snowfall had been lighter and the drifting less severe, the highway department, working all night, had cleared one lane each way.

Tucker drove straight south, through Evansville, across Kentucky, and on into Nashville. He turned east there, only a light covering of snow in the fields, and passed through Knoxville, on through the low mountain passes, and into North Carolina.

At Asheville, he checked into an old farmers' and merchants' hotel in the centre of town, sat by the window of his room looking down at the street and tried to sort through his alternatives.

After Whittaker was dead, when Tagge had driven Tucker and Thelma to the Burbank Airport to fly back to Costa Rica, Tucker had said, Thelma already on board the plane, he and Tagge standing at the foot of the boarding steps, 'I want to know if it's over.'

'The truth is, I don't know,' Tagge had said. 'The only kind of manoeuvre I ever feel good about is a one–man thing. The more people there are, the more chance there is for a screw–up. The bigger the noise, the bigger the stink, the more there is to cover up. And the man who chokes the most is the man who gave the original order. He always has the most at stake and the most to lose. If he panics, the dominoes start to fall.'

'How does that affect me?'

'I'm not sure it does. But it might. Let me put it this way. If I were you and I had a notion to disappear, in Brazil, for example, I think maybe I'd do it.'

So it was a contest now. Tucker knew that. A blood game. With only one question. How could he get to them before they decided the time was right to get to him?

All his instincts told him to force the action, to take the initiative, to drive to Washington and somehow find a way to isolate them, one to one, to do unto them before they had a chance to do unto him.

As much as that impulse fired him, some woodsman's instinct told him that he couldn't beat them on their own ground. They would be cushioned and guarded and surrounded there, able to manoeuvre, to run and hide in familiar corners. And retaliate when they chose to.

He needed a way, some way, to bring them to him, to make the contest, if not equal, at least a contest. But how could he do it? Sitting in his hotel room, looking down on the main street of Asheville, he didn't know the final answer. But he thought he knew a way to begin.

CHAPTER THIRTY–EIGHT

SITTING ACROSS THE desk from Kenneth Slauson, second vice–president of the Asheville–Buncombe National Bank, Tucker said, 'That's a cashier's cheque. It says, "Pay to Bearer", I'm the bearer. What do you need identification for?'

'That's our policy, Mister . . .'

'Tucker. My name's Roy Tucker.'

'Do you live in Asheville, Mr Tucker?'

'No. I don't. I'm staying at the Balfour Hotel down the street. Just checked in there yesterday.'

'Will you be here long?'

'A few days, I guess.'

'I see. What is your home address?'

'I don't have one right now. I've been out of the country for a while. I haven't decided yet where I want to live.'

'What was your last permanent address?'

'I lived in Chicago. North of there. A suburb called Lake Forest.'

'When was that?'

'Six years ago more or less. It's hard to remember. I've been moving around a lot.'

'What was your bank when you lived in Chicago?'

'Lake Forest. Not Chicago.'

'Yes. Where did you do your banking?'

'I didn't. The man I worked for paid me in cash. I didn't need any bank account.'

Mr Slauson excused himself then and walked into an office just behind his desk. He carried the cheque with him. In a moment he reappeared in the doorway and said, 'Can you come in, Mr Tucker?'

Inside the office, panelled and bright, Slauson introduced him to an older man, totally bald, the skin on his face thin and translucent, like old vellum, looking as if it had been grafted over a bad burn.

'This is Mr Pauley, our president. Have a chair, Mr Tucker.'

When Tucker sat down, Pauley said, 'Now . . . what can we do for you?'

'I want to cash that cheque you've got there.'

'May I see your driver's licence?'

'What for? That's a cashier's cheque.'

'That's true. We know all about cashier's cheques. But we don't cash any cheque without identification.'

'Well, that's a problem,' Tucker said slowly. 'I was in a bar in Knoxville night before last and I think somebody picked my pocket. Lifted my billfold clean as a whistle.'

'Are you saying you don't have any identification?'

'That's the way it looks,' Tucker said.

'Then I'm afraid we can't help you.'

'Why not? It's a bona fide cheque. You can see that. And I didn't steal it. You don't think I stole it, do you?'

'No. No one mentioned that.'

'What if I did steal it, it's still negotiable, isn't it? That's what a cashier's cheque is all about.'

'Technically, that's true. But not in our bank. Look at it from our standpoint. A gentleman we don't know gives us a rather rumpled cheque for a large amount of money. He has no home address and no identification and he wants immediate cash payment.'

'You do think I stole it, don't you?'

Pauley and Slauson exchanged a look. 'We're not policemen, Mr Tucker. This is a bank. We're business-men.'

'Good. Let's do some business. If you won't cash the cheque, then I'd like to open a savings account. I mean I can endorse it and open a savings account, can't I? If that cheque has no hold on it, if it clears and the money goes into Roy Tucker's account, then it's mine, isn't it?'

'Yes . . . under those circumstances . . .'

'And I can take it out any time I want to?'

Mr Pauley nodded. 'Once it's cleared with the issuing bank.'

'Good. Then you've got a new depositor. And here's what I want you to do so we don't lose any time. Call that bank in Washington so we can get it cleared today. If there's any problem at the other end tell the bank they can call Mr Thomas Reser at the White House. He sent me the cheque. Mr Reser is a special advisor to the President. When you mention the name Roy Tucker, he'll vouch for me. No question about it. You got all that?'

Slauson had been making notes as Tucker talked. He nodded his head and said, 'Yes, I think so.'

Tucker stood up. 'What time do you close this after-noon?'

'Three o'clock.'

'I'll call you at two–thirty. By then I expect to have a free and clean account for two hundred thousand dollars.'

'If there are no problems . . .' Pauley began.

'There won't be.'

CHAPTER THIRTY-NINE

THELMA'S PARENTS, DEKE and Nora Chester, thin and leathery, in their late fifties, looking ten years older, sat in the drafty kitchen of their two-storey frame house in Hazelwood, North Carolina, early evening, the remains of supper in front of them, Tucker seated across the table drinking coffee out of a china mug.

Nora was crying. She'd cried earlier when Tucker first arrived. Now she was crying again.

'It hurts me to think of Thelma being taken like that. I reckon they've got some awful diseases down there in those hot, tacky countries.'

'The doctor said it was plain old pneumonia and she wasn't strong enough to fight it,' Tucker said. 'She got sick on a Wednesday and by Friday noon she was dead.'

'She never was a strong kid. She was always kind of the runt of the litter. But she had more spunk and ginger than all the rest of them put together. Going to work so young the way she did. And heading off to Chicago next thing we knew just like she was a grown-up.'

Nora blew her nose. 'It really hurts me all over to think of her laid away in some foreign country I never even heard of before. No way we can look after her grave or anything.'

'It's all taken care of just fine,' Tucker said. 'Perpetual care, they call it. It's a beautiful place where she's buried. And it's tended and cared for just perfect.'

136

Tucker had come there to lie, to tell her parents the truth in only one sense, to tell them Thelma was dead, but to lie about all the other details, to soften the edges, to make them feel as good as possible about her and about themselves.

'She wasn't one to write much,' Nora went on. 'None of our kids is worth a nickel when it comes to writing home. But we'd hear scrips and scraps from other people once in a while, from folks around here who'd moved up to Chicago. And once in a coon's age we'd get a card from Thelma's cousin Fay out in California. She's a reader, Fay is, keeps track of everything. She's the one that let us know when that man Thelma was married to got killed and you and her went to the pen for it. Thelma never wrote at all after that. I guess she thought she'd shamed us by going to jail.'

Tucker lied about all that too. He'd worked it out in his head as he drove south from Chicago.

'That was a big mistake,' he said. 'The law made a big mistake. Just as soon as they found out about it, they pardoned me, let me out of jail slick as a whistle, and paid me a few thousand dollars to boot because they'd sent Thelma and me to jail for something we never did. That was the money we used to go down to Central America, to get us a little place in Costa Rica where nobody would know what had happened to us. And where we could live cheap.

'We thought we'd farm a little, truck–farm mostly, raise produce and the like, milk a few goats, and feed some hogs. And we talked about having some kids.'

'It's a goddamned shame,' Deke said. 'That's what it is.' He was a short, grizzled man, bone–thin, a crutch by his chair, his left leg cut off at the knee. 'You're the one we heard was dead. Fay sent us a clipping from some paper saying you'd been shot some place up there in Canada.'

'I never figured out what that was all about,' Tucker said. 'Some mix–up in the prison records, I guess. Right after I was pardoned and turned loose, a couple of guys broke out of Hobart and the papers said it was me. They got it balled up good. They even said, some of the papers, that I was in on that mess when they shot President Whittaker out in California. All they'd have had to do was check a little and they'd have found out I was in Costa Rica all that time.'

'Can't trust the papers,' Deke said. 'We don't even take one. Can't trust half of what you see printed. Or the TV either. You can look around and see we don't own one, I wouldn't have one on the place, but I see one every so often in a store or a tavern or some place. And I guarantee you I wouldn't trust any of those people for a minute. Or anything they say.'

CHAPTER FORTY

After Tagge and Pine had manoeuvred Tucker out of prison, they let him fly alone on commercial jets from Chicago to Mexico to Honduras to Costa Rica, a loose rein, no supervision or surveillance. Thelma was their security. They had already taken her to Costa Rica and Tucker knew it.

There had been a waiting period then, a parenthesis, a reward, Tucker and Thelma alone in a splendid house overlooking the sea, together for the first time in more than five years, since that day in the Marion County Jail, their first time ever together as man and wife, all day and all night together, time to talk and listen, to touch and sleep and be silent, to wake up together and have breakfast in the sun.

'It's like a miracle,' Thelma said. 'I can't believe you're here. I can't believe either one of us is here. Is this where we're going to live now?'

'That's right. Slick and fancy.'

'I just can't swallow it all. It's too much and too good. I can't believe it. You don't know what it was like for me when you wrote that letter three years ago and told me not to come visit you at Hobart or write any more letters.'

'That doesn't matter now, does it?'

'I guess not. Everything's perfect now. But I still don't understand what you were thinking of.'

'I told you,' he said. 'I wrote it all in that letter. It was one thing when you were in jail, too. But once they'd let you out, when you were paroled and free to lead some kind of a regular life, I couldn't take the idea of you waiting around all that time for me. I didn't want to hang you up like that.'

'You're crazy, Roy. That was what we settled on when we got married. It didn't matter to me.'

'But it mattered to me. That's what I meant.'

'I wasn't doing it for you,' she said. 'I was doing it for me. I just wanted us to be together no matter how long it took or anything.' She put her arms around him. 'And now it's happened. Like some miracle out of a Bible-class story.' Then, 'How long you think it'll be before your new trial comes up?'

That was the lie he had told her, that Tagge and Pine had also told her, before they brought her to Costa Rica to wait for him, that they had arranged a new trial, manslaughter the charge, instead of first degree murder.

'Not long, I guess,' Tucker told her. 'They're working on it now.'

'They said that when they get it changed around to manslaughter you'll be up for parole right away because you've already put in more than five years.'

'That's right. That's the idea.'

'God, we're lucky,' she said. 'I always thought we were unlucky. But now I think we're the luckiest people I ever heard of.'

139

'Yeah, we're lucky all right.'

He wondered how long it would be before she guessed the truth, before she realised what kind of bargain he had made, what the price would be, how long before he realised it himself, before the moment came when they would tell him exactly what they wanted him to do.

At the end of his first meeting with Tagge, in the locked room down the hall from the warden's office, Tucker had said, 'Let me get this straight. You want to help me and you want nothing from me in return. Is that it?'

'No. That's not it. We will definitely want something in return.'

CHAPTER FORTY–ONE

TUCKER STAYED ALL night with Thelma's parents. They insisted on it. After a long time at the table in the kitchen and another two hours drinking whisky and water in the living room, all of Thelma's baby pictures, school diplomas, and high–school mementoes brought out, discussed, and examined, her mother made up the cot in the corner and Tucker slept there.

The next morning after breakfast, Deke drove him up into the hills five miles north of Hazelwood and showed him the family place, the little house in a grove of trees where Thelma had been born.

'All my people was farmers,' Deke said. 'Nora's too. All I was ever fit for was to farm. But once I got this leg

140

blowed off, I wasn't fit for nothing. More than twenty–five years now since we had to give up the place and take over that one–horse store in Hazelwood and I ain't had a day in all that time that I didn't feel miserable and not worth a damn.

'I guess maybe if we'd had boys instead of all those girls we could have stuck it out. I could have made it, I reckon, if I'd had just one strong boy to stay home and help me out. It wasn't that much land. Eighty acres, a little over. And half of that was woods and pasture. But the only boy I had was born car–crazy. Dead–set on being a mechanic from the time he could wiggle. He was working part–time in the Standard station over at Waynesville when he was twelve. And soon as his sixteenth birthday came along, he quit school, hitch–hiked all the way up to Winston–Salem, and got himself a job in the Chevy garage there. Up till then we'd been just squeezing by, me doing what work I could and him taking care of the rest. But after he took off and his sisters all married city men, not one in the bunch that knowed the difference between a manure fork and a butter churn, after that, I had to give up, sell off the place for whatever I could get, and scratch around for some other way to make ends meet.

'I got screwed good when I sold my land and I got screwed when I bought the store. Sold too cheap, bought too dear. But that's what happens when you're squeezed into a corner. You got to make the best deal you can and live with it. But I'll tell you one thing – a man that was brought up to take care of stock and grow crops ain't ever gonna feel right about sacking up soup beans and slicing baloney. It's no kind of a life you can feel good about. I've thought to myself many a time that fucking Jap would have done me a favour if he'd hit me square–on and put me out of my misery.'

'How'd it happen?'

'I was on a destroyer down in the Marianas. Seaman second class on a gun crew. We were pounding the piss out of them, sinking their carriers right and left, shooting down everything they threw at us. Then one day they started that kamikaze shit. You ever heard of that?'

'Suicide pilots they called them.'

141

'That's it. Those crazy bastards were ready to kill themselves just to make a hit. I never could get that straight in my head, how a man could climb into a plane and know he was going out there and blow himself up. I mean I like a good scrap as much as the next guy, at least I did when I had two legs to get around on, but what kind of a fight is it when one guy is ready to kill himself just to hurt somebody else? I mean war don't make any sense to start with, guys on both sides trying to kill people they don't even know. But it makes a hell of a lot more sense than a bunch of assholes killing themselves.'

'I read someplace it was like a religion,' Tucker said. 'They figured it was a good thing to die like that. If they could do some damage for their side, they thought one man staying alive wasn't that important. I guess that's the way they must have looked at it.'

'Well, whatever they had in their heads they sure made us bleed. We took four direct hits that day. All in twenty minutes time. Four zeros blew up on our deck. And the last one ripped my leg off. The CO said I was lucky. Three guys from my crew, they had to pick up the pieces in a bucket. But it didn't feel like luck to me. I never seen a man with an empty pants–leg who thought he was lucky.'

He turned off the road, drove up a rutted lane, and stopped in front of a two–storey frame house, the windows boarded up, the front door hanging crooked on its hinges, the roof sagging over the porch, shingles ripped off and scattered on the ground.

'A big cattle outfit over in Charlotte bought the place from the man I sold it to. They fenced it all with barbed wire and they're using the whole eighty acres for pasture. Nothing's been planted or harvested here for fifteen or twenty years.

'They cut down the fruit trees and bulldozed the barns and the chicken house. They even filled in the well. So it's no farm at all any more. Just a big fenced–in pen for running cattle. Makes you sick just to look at it.

'When I saw they wasn't making any use of the house, I tried to rent it off of them. I figured Nora and me could live here and keep a few chickens and still drive into Hazelwood and mind the store every day. But they said they didn't want anybody living in the house. They'd rather just have it sit here and go to rot the way it's doing. Sons-of-bitches. They don't understand anything.'

Inside the empty house, Tucker followed along from room to room, everything neglected and dilapidated, beetles and field mice scurrying across the floor, as Deke inspected the kitchen and the sitting room and a downstairs bedroom that opened out on the back porch, then climbed the stairs to prowl the four small bedrooms on the second floor.

'This here was Thelma's room. She was born downstairs in her mother's bed but this was her room from the time she was weaned. She was only three or four, I guess, when I had to give up the place but this is where she slept when she was little. You can see we left some of her stuff here, her crib and that table and chair her brother made her. And that little painted sled. I made that.

'Thellie was our last one so we didn't see any reason to haul a lot of baby stuff around with us when we moved. Had no more use for it and didn't have much of a place to store it anyhow. And it's kind of nice to see one of the rooms with a few sticks of furniture left in it when I drive out here once in a while to snoop around. Downstairs it's nothing but bats and mice and raccoon shit. But up here in Thelma's room you can still get the idea that maybe somebody lived here once.'

Late that morning, Tucker drove back into Asheville. He left his car behind the hotel and walked down the street to the bank. On the way he stopped at the Woolworth store on the square and bought a small cardboard suitcase covered with imitation leather.

Inside the bank, when he sat down across from Mr Slauson at his desk, Slauson said, 'We expected to hear from you yesterday afternoon.'

'I thought you might need some extra time.'

'As a matter of fact we didn't.' He opened his centre drawer, took out a brown bankbook and slid it across the desk top to Tucker. 'There you are. You now have a pass-book account at our regular interest rates. If you'd like to tie up the money for a longer period we can offer you a higher rate, of course.'

'No problem with the cheque then?'

'None at all. The Washington bank called us back an hour after we contacted them and authorised us to release the total amount to you.'

'To Roy Tucker?'

'That's right.'

'Did you give them Mr Reser's name like I told you to?'

'Yes. We did exactly as you instructed.'

'Good.' Tucker picked up the suitcase he'd bought and put in on Slauson's desk. 'Here's what I want,' he said. 'I'd like to leave a thousand dollars in the account. The rest of the money I'll take in cash. Twenties and fifties. Put it in this bag and I'll pick it up before you close this afternoon.'

CHAPTER FORTY–TWO

BEING IN NORTH Carolina, seeing Asheville and Hazel-wood, Tucker brought Thelma into painful sharp focus again. He saw her face everywhere he looked, heard her soft country voice, felt her hands again, light as small birds. She had been dead for only a few weeks but in some way the time seemed long and immeasurable. In another aching way he felt her presence, her heartbeat, her breath as though she had just, on the instant, left the room.

The memory of those last tormented days in Costa Rica he blotted out. After Whittaker was dead. And Tagge. Still lying to Thelma about the details of what had happened in California, he had tried to persuade her that they were liberated now, free to walk the beaches, free to sit on their terrace at the edge of the rain forest and look out across the ocean. And she pretended that she was persuaded. But there was a sense of despair that neither of them could dispel. It misted through the house like a sea fog. When she was killed, when he found her dead and crumpled in the road, he was stunned and shattered, babbling like a lunatic. But he wasn't surprised. He had gambled for his freedom and lost. The best he could expect now was permanent chaos. He knew that clearly. And Thelma had known it too.

But before that final heartsick return to Costa Rica, during their previous stay there, together again after more than five years apart, hoping for the best, devouring the moments like jungle fruit, devouring each other, eating and drinking and lying naked on the bed through long sultry afternoons, in that time, for those brief days, they had swooped and soared to all the high meadows a man and a woman can visit together.

'My God,' she had said, 'if we only had these days, in this place, we'd be rich, wouldn't we? I think we would. I feel as if I straddled a white horse and rode straight up to heaven.'

But she didn't expect it to end there. And neither did he. Not then. Not in those days of ecstasy and triumph. They thought it was a beginning. Lots more to come. Good food, soft nights, and warm beds to sleep in. They had discussed it endlessly. Thelma had painted a verdant glowing landscape of what their life would be. And as he drove now through the roads of North Carolina, those were the words that Tucker remembered, as though they were real, as though they had come true.

'We can buy a house up in the hills somewhere not far from Hazelwood. Or we can build us one if we want to. Make it just the way we want it to be. But to tell you the

145

truth, I have a soft spot for old places, houses that have been around a while, that are used to people living in them. Kids and cats and dogs and chickens in the back yard. I like a place that's broken-in. You know what I mean? With flowers and bushes all ready to bloom as soon as the spring rains come down.'

At that time he hadn't told her about the two hundred thousand dollars in his name in the Puntarenas Bank, hadn't told her that the deed to their oceanview house was also in his name. It was still too new to him. He couldn't believe it. It was almost a burden somehow, one he wasn't willing to share with her.

So her plans were small-scale, keyed to her background and his. Manageable, believable plans, the kind working people make.

'We can both get jobs in Asheville. I'm sure of that. We'll live cheap and save a lot of money and we'll have enough for a down payment on a place before you know it. My folks will help us out. They'll be glad to. They don't have much money but we can get our groceries for cost there at the store. I can't wait for you to see Hazelwood and the country around there. The way I remember it, it looks a lot like that part of West Virginia that you come from. You'll take one look at it and say, "I'm home." I'll bet a dollar that's how you'll feel.

'I think that area's the best bet for us. As far as finding a house, I mean. I hear a lot of the people have pulled up and left. Gone to the city to find work. Or people have just died off and their kids don't want to live out in the country. So there'll be places to buy. I'm sure of that. My dad knows those counties, Haywood and Henderson and Buncombe and Jackson, like his pocket. If anybody's property is up for sale he'll know about it.

'Then once we get our own place we'll have a great old time fixing it up. Paint and paper and a few nails and you can change a house altogether. We'll plant a garden and keep some chickens and if we've got the room we'll feed a few pigs so we'll always have fresh pork in the freezer. And Dad will show you how to sugar-cure it if you don't already know. He can cure hams and bacon so you never tasted anything like it.

'And all the time you and I will be able to keep whatever jobs we find in Asheville and drive back and forth every day. Mom can help out with the kids when we have some and we'll have ourselves a fine life. I wouldn't be surprised if we could take over Dad's store, too, when he's ready to pack it in. Then we'd really have it made. Both of us home all day, working together, with no more driving into Asheville. Wouldn't that be perfect? And besides we'd get everything from the store at cost. Whatever we need. I tell you, Tucker, we're going to slide right down the rainbow.'

Listening to her, he had allowed himself to believe. Even later, against all logic, he had continued to hope and believe for as long as he could. Some lonely, yearning part of him had stubbornly planned and hoped and believed right to the very end. Only when he picked her up at the edge of the road and carried her home, only then did all the hope and sweetness tear loose inside him and gust up out of his throat in a jagged cry of hatred and heartbreak and nothing at all left to hold on to.

CHAPTER FORTY–THREE

TUCKER ATE LUNCH in the Balfour Hotel coffee shop. Ham and beans, cornbread and coffee. Then he walked out to the parking lot, a light snow beginning to sift down, unlocked his car trunk, took out the cardboard carton Applegate had sent him from Wisconsin, and carried it up in the elevator to his room. He cut the twine, sliced through the packing tape, ripped open the carton, and lifted out the garrison bag, khaki–coloured canvas, his name and serial number stencilled on it in black.

Unlocking the padlock with the key Applegate had mailed ahead to Chicago, Tucker set the bag on the luggage stand at the foot of the bed and began to take out the articles packed inside. Mostly, the bag was filled with clothes. Socks and underwear, shirts and pants and ties. An olive–drab sweater, a knit cap, two web belts, handkerchiefs, a muffler, a fatigue cap, an overseas cap, a field jacket, and a poncho.

Tucked away in one corner was a pocket–size photo album. He flipped through it. A snapshot of his sister and her first two kids, another one of him and Applegate standing outside a bar in Yokohama, several pictures of Japanese girls, and a blonde girl in a nurse's uniform, Agnes Wheeler. She'd been stationed at the field hospital outside Longbinh.

At the bottom of the bag, wrapped in an undershirt, he found the North Vietnamese bayonet he'd won in a poker game in the orderly room. And a canvas sack with four Vietcong grenades inside it, small and smooth as turkey eggs, half the size of his fist. He laid them out in a row on top of the bed with the bayonet beside them.

He found Applegate's tape recorder then, wrapped in a pair of pants, wedged into a corner of the bag. It was flat and rectangular, two inches thick, the length and width of a business envelope. A white card was scotch–taped to the top with a note scrawled on it.

Roy.
Listen to this tape. I think it will answer some questions.

Applegate

Tucker walked over to the window and sat down, the tape recorder on a low table in front of him. Looking at

Applegate's handwriting, spontaneous and immediate, he kept hearing Corinne's voice. 'If he'd never met you he wouldn't be dead.'

At last, almost against his will, dreading in some way to hear whatever was on the tape, apprehensive of the paradox, Applegate dead and Applegate speaking, Tucker reached out and pressed the forward button. A light flicked on, a small, orange dot, the tape crawled forward, and Applegate's voice, full presence, as clear as if he were in the room, came smoothly out of the built-in speaker.

'Well, Roy . . . here we are. Or should I say, here *I* am. It's very nice here. You'd like this place. Ten acres in the woods on the edge of a lake. And an old sprawling house that Corinne's grandfather built in 1875. Stone and timber. As solid as a blockhouse. As a matter of fact, it looks like a blockhouse, a good place to fight off Indians. It's all fixed up now, of course. Water and electricity and gas and central heating. All those things we've decided we can't live without. So I'm sitting here with my shoes off and my feet up. It's snowing outside and cold as a bitch but I'm warm and comfortable. Having a beer and a cheese sandwich like a man on a backwoods vacation.

'The catch is it's *not* a vacation. I'm not sure what you'd call it but I know I'm on the run. A car followed me up here from Chicago and there's been somebody watching the house ever since. I guess they think I know too much. Well . . . they don't know the half of it. If they knew how much I know, at least how much I think I know, I'd be buried by now.

'Ever since I saw you in Chicago I've been racking my brain, trying to remember the bits and pieces I picked up from Tagge through the years, trying to stick it all together in some way that makes sense. Now I think I've got it worked out. It scares hell out of me but it all hangs together.

'Keep in mind that magazine clipping I sent you about the Interworld Alliance. I think that's the key to everything. The other key is Reser.

'Let's start with Reser. Tagge has been talking to me

149

about him for years. He thought he was a fool. But ambitious and dangerous.

'First of all, that story Henemyer told you, about the South Vietnamese kickback to Washington to keep the war going, was true, I think. But the man with the Zurich bank account was not Whittaker. It was Reser. Remember he was Chief of Staff under Johnson and after he retired from the Pentagon he was Whittaker's bosom buddy and military advisor. So he was right there all the time with his hand on the throttle, pressuring Congress for more planes, more rockets, more dollars.

'And when Interworld handpicked the boob who followed Whittaker into the White House, Reser must have been on the selection committee. That's what Whittaker was driving at when he said we had to be afraid of the industrial and military complex.

'All right . . . so far we're talking about dirty politics: bribes, kickbacks and all the rest of it. So what else is new? Nothing unusual about the oil men and the bankers and the steel men and the auto–makers trying to get their foot in the door at the White House. Business as usual. Everybody expects that. But why did Whittaker have to be killed? He's a private man, not too bright, and he's out of office. Fishing and playing golf and accepting honorary degrees. But popular as hell still with the people. Good old Neal. Dangerous to assassinate a popular man like that. Gets people very mad and very nervous. So why do it? Only one reason. He knew something. Not something past, but something future. There was something rotten in the game plan, something big and dirty in the works. So Whittaker passed the word along. "Scrub the whole thing or I'll blow the whistle."

'So there they were. He couldn't be muscled and he couldn't be bought so they had to kill him. That's where you came in. Tagge came to me, I sent him to you, and they got the job done.

'So now Whittaker's dead. And most of the people who know how he died are dead, too. Just you and me left. And Henemyer and Reser. Because I have a hunch the buck stops with Reser. The I.A. and the White House may be tickled to death that Whittaker's out of the way but I'd be surprised if they were in on it. Before the fact or after. I think Reser engineered that by himself, with the help of whatever cronies and right–wing idiots he could enlist, using his power at the top as a wedge, using the "oval office" and "national security" as slogans whenever anybody hesitated. How he got Tagge to go along I'll never know but everybody's got a body buried somewhere and I guess Tagge was no exception.

'What about Reser? I've been thinking a lot about him. What gives him his power? What makes him a key figure in this organisation that controls trillions of dollars and most of the major industries outside the Soviet–Chinese bloc? He's not a brilliant man. He wasn't even a great general. So what is it? What's he got?

'There's only one answer to that . . . the Arabs. He's the only man they trust. The only man we've got who commands respect there. He's a small time, second–rate son–of–a–bitch but the Arabs love him. So . . . next step . . . it follows that the Interworld Alliance must be up to something fishy with the Arabs. That means oil. But what's the game and how did Whittaker tie in? Well . . . it's all right on the front page of the newspapers and it has been for weeks. I was just too dumb to make the connection till I got up here by myself and started thinking about it. It's so obvious I almost missed it.

'Anyway, here's what happened. Two or three weeks ago some White House stooge calmly announced that the President is considering a massive arms programme for the Middle East – planes and tanks and munitions to all the key Arab states. When that clicked in my head, when I started to connect it to Reser and the I.A. and Whittaker, I remembered something Tagge had told me three or four years ago.

'He said there were people in Washington who wanted to arm the Arabs so they would start a full–scale war with Israel and wipe it off the map. The theory was that the Arabs would get power-hungry then, choose up sides, and start a war among themselves. In the chaos, our country, with the backing of Japan, West Germany, and all the so–called peace–loving anti–Communist nations, would step in as peacemakers. When the smoke cleared a complicated protectorate government would be set up. All this to preserve peace and guarantee oil production. A temporary solution, including the decision to return control of the oil fields to the international companies who had done the original Mideast drilling and development. *Temporary*. But it would turn out to be permanent for as long as the Arab fields pump oil. Tagge laughed about it when he told me. Said it could never happen. I say it's happening now.

'Reser speaks at the United Nations next week and two days later he goes to Saudi Arabia to meet with the Arab leaders. Arms for peace, they call it. But I guarantee you that in less that two years the Middle East will be a river of blood, and Israel will be a field of cinders. That's what Whittaker knew. That's what he couldn't let happen. And that's why they had to kill him.

'I may not have all the details right. But I know I'm close. Do you see what's at stake, Roy? More money than we can count. Control of the world's oil supply. And incredible power. Military and political. You want to guess what Whittaker's life was worth in that equation? Thelma's life? Yours and mine? *Zero*. A little less than that.

'Sometime tonight I'm slipping out of here. I'm going to lose myself. When it's safe for Corinne and the kids to be with me, I'll send for them. But for now the only way I know to protect them is to stay as far away as I can. So that's what I'm going to do.

As for you, I know what's in your head. And all I can say is . . . *don't do it*. Don't even think about it. You're one guy by yourself and you don't have a chance. Getting yourself killed won't solve anything. And it won't change anything that's already happened. Trust me and listen to me. Just disappear, the way I'm doing . . .'

The tape rolled on, making a soft slithering sound. Tucker let it run to the end of the cassette. When it stopped turning, he switched off the machine.

CHAPTER FORTY–FOUR

AT TWO FORTY–FIVE in the afternoon, Tucker went to the bank to get his money. When Slauson handed him the suitcase he said, 'Just sign this withdrawal slip.' Then, 'Don't you want to count it?'

'Did you count it?'

'Yes, I did.'

'That's good enough for me.'

He drove out to Hazelwood then and found Nora Chester by herself in the store, sitting by the wood stove, knitting, a man's wool sweater over her shoulders.

'Deke's down at the Legion hall,' she said. 'He plays darts down there two or three times a week. He used to be a lunatic card player, hearts and euchre mostly. Now it's darts. You can stop by there if you want to. He'd be tickled to see you.'

'No, that's all right,' Tucker said. 'I'll see him later. I just wanted to drop off a couple of bags here. Thought maybe you'd keep an eye on them for me.'

'Be glad to.'

'I've got a fair–sized garrison bag and a little suitcase out in the car. Where can I put them?'

'Upstairs, I reckon, is the best place. There's a walk–in hall closet at the top of the stairs. Plenty of room up there. And there's a key to it if your stuff needs to be locked up.'

He carried the two bags upstairs, put them against the wall at the back of the closet, locked the door, and left the key with Mrs Chester on his way out.

'I'll put that key right here in the change drawer,' she said. 'At the back. Underneath the fives and tens. If you should come past for your suitcases and I'm not here for one reason or another, just tell Deke where I hid the key and he can dig it out for you.'

Tucker drove back to Asheville then, pulled up in front of the courthouse, parked at the curb, and walked in the entrance marked POLICE. At the end of a long corridor, he found an office with a painted sign over the door, LT MORTON BAINES, CHIEF OF DETECTIVES.

Inside the office a heavy, grey-haired woman sat at a bare desk facing the door, erect in her chair, her fingers laced loosely together on the desk top.

'I'd like to see Lieutenant Baines,' Tucker said.

'Is it police business?'

'I guess it is. My name's Roy Tucker. I broke out of prison in Indiana last October. I want to turn myself in.'

CHAPTER FORTY-FIVE

THREE HOURS LATER, early evening in Washington DC, the street clogged with three days of snow, the air damp and foggy, Henemyer sat in the office of Frank Stokely in the J. Edgar Hoover Building.

'I remembered you'd asked for surveillance on a man named Brookshire in Chicago so I figured there might be a connection.'

'It's the same guy,' Henemyer said. 'We knew he was in Asheville.'

'What's the story?'

'He's with Treasury. Secret Service. Executive Security. That's all I know. We bump into each other once in a while.'

'Why did you want him tailed?'

'I can't tell you.'

'Knock it off, will you? I'm not the enemy, for Christ's sake. You're not doing me a favour. I'm doing you one. We had a routine request from Asheville. If you want to play beanbag with me I'll just handle it as routine and we'll forget it.'

'What kind of routine request? What do they want?'

'Fingerprint check. They've got a guy who says he's an escaped convict named Tucker. But he paid his hotel bill with traveller's cheques signed Martin Brookshire. And he had a car he'd rented in Chicago using the same name. So they took his prints and wired them to us to find out who he is. He says Roy Tucker. They're not sure.'

'That's who he is,' Henemyer said.

'You just said he was Brookshire.'

'That's a cover name.'

'You mean there are two Roy Tuckers who got out of jail in Indiana two months ago?'

'No. Just one. This is him.'

'What about the one that was shot up in Canada?'

'Frank, you're getting into corners I can't get you out of. Reser's unit is up to its ears in that Whittaker investigation and you know it. You're one of the few people who do know it. So give us a break. He's got clearance from the mountain top and nothing is supposed to leak. Not to you. Not to anybody.'

'I'm not trying to pump you. I just want to know what you want to do about this friend of yours in Asheville. I'll tell them he's Jesse James if that will make you happy.'

CHAPTER FORTY–SIX

'WHAT DID YOU tell Stokely?' Reser said.

'I said we thought there might be some connection between the Hobart prison break and Whittaker's assassination.'

'Jesus, you can't confide in those bastards. They all kiss Jack Anderson's ass.'

'I didn't tell him anything that hasn't been in a dozen newspapers already. I just massaged it around a little. I told him Tucker is working with us to furnish evidence against the real shooter, the guy who was killed in Canada. I said we'd been moving him around a lot and he was using the name Martin Brookshire.'

They were sitting in a corner of the lobby of the Hay-Adam Hotel, just before midnight.

'I don't like it,' Reser said. 'That redneck bastard really sticks in my throat. From the first day I saw him. Guys like that give you nothing but grief. Hard–headed, stubborn sons–of–bitches. What the hell is he up to? First, he pulls a number at some bank down there. Now he's turned himself in to the police.'

'He's a dumb guy, Tom. He doesn't know what he's doing.'

'Yeah, I know. At least that's what you keep saying. But every time we turn around he's lit another fire.'

'No more. I think we have to deal with him now. I'm going down to Asheville in the morning. I'll take care of it myself.'

'What about the Asheville police?'

'I already talked to the Commissioner down there. I called him from Stokely's office. I explained that it was our problem and we would handle it. Stokely talked to him, too.'

'You have to be careful with those local guys. You give them too much attention and then they start to get ambitious . . .'

Henemyer shook his head. 'Stokely told him the fingerprints his people sent through belong to Brookshire. And I told him Brookshire works for me. I'll fill in some details when I pick Tucker up tomorrow. They'll be satisfied, I promise you.'

When they stood inside the front entrance waiting for their cars to be brought up, Reser said, 'I want you with me when I go up to New York Monday. I don't want anything to interfere with that.'

'No problem. I'll be back in Washington tomorrow evening.'

'What time? I may have to leave a message for you at the airport.'

Henemyer took an airline ticket out of his pocket, checked the inside flap. 'Eastern,' he said. 'Flight 216. Gets in Dulles at eight forty–five.'

'Good. I'll talk to you tomorrow night one way or another.'

Reser stayed inside the warm waiting–area watching through the windows as Henemyer went outside, got into his car, and drove away. As his own car pulled up at the entrance, Reser turned up his collar, pushed through the revolving door, hurried down the hotel steps in the damp cold, and got into the back seat. Frank Stokely sat there waiting for him.

Reser switched on the speaker connection and spoke to his driver. 'We'll stop for a second at the Hoover Building parking lot. Then I'm going home.'

As the car pulled out into the street, turned left and picked up speed, Reser said to Stokely, 'He'll be on Eastern flight 216. Dulles. Eight forty–five tomorrow evening.'

'No problem.'

'You sound like Henemyer. If it's not a fucking earth-quake, it's not a problem.'

'There's a guy driving down from Montreal. He's the best. Henemyer will have a cardiac arrest on his way home from the airport.'

CHAPTER FORTY–SEVEN

LATE THE FOLLOWING morning Henemyer sat in an office in Asheville's courthouse with Chief of Police Gavin and Lieutenant Baines.

'I could tell you some fancy stories,' Henemyer said. 'Or I could hide behind a screen of "national security" and not tell you anything. But I'd rather tell you the truth. As much as I can. We have a lot of respect for the local law-enforcement people around the country and we want them to have the same respect for us. All of us have a job to do and more often than not we can help each other.'

He leaned forward, plucked a cigarette out of a metal box on Gavin's desk, and lit it. 'As I mentioned before I'm not free to say what Brookshire's been working on for us. But I can tell you it's a top priority thing and we've all been under a lot of pressure, Brookshire most of all. He's been on the move for weeks. Not much sleep. In and out of the country. Never getting home to see his family. It's been a rough session. And from what you've told me, the strain must be getting to him. But we know how to handle that. We'll see that he gets a good rest and whatever treatment he needs. He'll be good as new in a month or so.'

Twenty minutes later, an officer brought Tucker's rented car around from the police parking lot to the side entrance of the courthouse. Henemyer and Tucker came out and got into the car, Tucker behind the wheel, and drove off.

As they pulled away from the courthouse, Henemyer opened his coat and jacket to show the butt of a .22 automatic in his flat belt holster.

Tucker glanced at it and said, 'You made your point. Where we going?'

'I've never been down here before. I'd like to take a look at some of the country. Where does this road go?'

'Straight west. Then south. If you stay on it long enough, you end up in Georgia.'

'I don't want to go to Georgia, do you?'

'I've got a hunch my vote doesn't count.'

'Sure it does,' Henemyer said. Then, 'Let's just drive on west a little way. If we see some pretty country, we'll turn off and look it over.'

The road was slick. It had rained the night before, on top of the snow, and the temperature had dropped through the morning. Tucker drove carefully, west through Enka and Canton and Clyde.

'A couple of things I don't understand,' Henemyer said. 'What was all that business at the bank?'

'What do you mean?'

'You had Brookshire's identification. You've used it everyplace else. All you had to do was show it and they'd have honoured that cheque in a minute.'

'I never thought of that,' Tucker said. 'I thought it was against the law if you didn't use your real name at a bank.'

'Bullshit. What you really wanted was to shake us up a little.'

'Why would I do that?'

'Then you decided to go to the police. What the hell was that supposed to prove?'

'Asheville's a pretty dull town. I thought maybe I could stir it up some.'

159

'You're crazy. Do you know that? You don't know when you're well off. At first I thought you were dumb. Now I think you're nuts.'

'That's not what they said when I went to prison the first time. They gave me a bunch of tests and they decided I was a very well–balanced guy. Said I should have been an accountant. Or a lawyer maybe.'

Henemyer shook his head. 'All you know is head–knocking. You're always looking for some kind of a fight. I don't know how you stayed alive in prison.'

'I had lots of fights. I even won a few.'

'Did you really think you could keep pushing and we wouldn't do anything about it?'

'Not exactly. I thought if I kept pushing you might come down here so we could have a talk.'

'About what?'

'About my wife mostly. I want to know who was driving that car. I want to know who gave the order to have her killed.'

'Jesus . . . are you still on that? I told you . . . that was an accident. We had nothing to do with it. I told you that before. Why would I lie about it? It's all over now.'

'Not for me it's not.'

'Forget it, Tucker. You've screwed yourself to the wall. Just keep your eyes on the road and drive the car.' Henemyer slipped the automatic out of its holster and rebuttoned his jacket and overcoat. 'And don't give yourself a headache thinking about all the things you could have done and didn't. You did plenty. If we'd have known the trouble you were going to cause us, you'd still be sitting in your cell back there at Hobart.'

Just south of Waynesville, Henemyer said, 'Slow down a little. You see that road up ahead? Turn right there.'

'That's rough going.'

'Don't worry about it.'

It was the road he'd driven up with Deke, the one that led through the hills to the old Chester place. As the car slipped and slewed along the rutted road, Tucker said, 'You fixing to bury me up here or just leave me for the coons?'

'Neither one. I'll deliver you back to the Asheville police. All neat and legal. I'll tell them you grabbed my gun away from me and shot yourself. They think you're a little psycho anyway. They'll believe whatever I tell them.'

The road narrowed at the crown of a thirty–yard downgrade, a deep gully at the bottom where the road veered sharply left.

'All right,' Henemyer said, 'let's turn the car around.'

Tucker slowed down and stopped, the motor idling smoothly. 'The road's too narrow here. We'll get stuck in the drifts if I try to come around.'

'There's a wide place down there where the road slants off. You can turn there.'

Tucker shifted into low then and eased down the hill, his eyes fixed on a bare gravel spot halfway down where the snow had blown away before it could pack solid and freeze over. When he reached that rough bare spot, when he felt his back wheels touch and find traction, he jerked the gears out of low, jammed his foot down on the accelerator, and felt the car rocket forward. At the same instant, he swung his right arm like a club and his fist smashed into Henemyer's face as the car tobogganed off the end of the road, hung free in the air, then plummeted to the floor of the ravine, half–rolled on its right side, and smashed into a thick grove of hickory trees.

Tucker, bracing himself with his arms and legs, felt the full collision shock in his knees and shoulders and elbows but kept his head from hitting the windshield. Henemyer, stunned from the blow to his face, fell forward on impact, cracked the glass with his head and smashed his nose against the padded top of the dashboard.

Tucker slumped behind the steering wheel, heavy and hurting, the ignition switched off, waiting for his head to clear. At last he reached across to the car floor, picked up the automatic and slid it into his overcoat pocket. Then he got out of the car, slowly and painfully, and stumbled away from the wreck, through the ankle–deep, hard–crusted snow, half carrying, half dragging Henemyer along with him.

CHAPTER FORTY–EIGHT

AN HOUR LATER, when Henemyer came to, he was sitting on the floor in an upstairs bedroom in the old Chester farm-house. His legs were spread wide in front of him on the floor, with his back leaning against the narrow end of the baby crib, his left wrist tied to one leg and his right wrist to the other.

There was a long cut on his forehead, another one on his chin, and his nose was purple and swollen, dried blood crusted on his cheeks and his upper lip.

When he opened his eyes, when he shook his head and his vision began to come clear, he saw Tucker sitting on a straight chair, a child's chair, five feet in front of him. The automatic lay on the floor beside the chair.

'Jesus . . . what are you doing?'

Tucker didn't answer, didn't move.

'I'm freezing to death,' Henemyer said. 'It's fucking freezing in here. Are you gonna let me sit here and freeze to death? My head is killing me, for Christ's sake, and I'm freezing. What do you want?'

Still Tucker didn't answer. He sat with his forearms resting on his knees, staring at Henemyer.

'What do you want?'

'I told you what I want,' Tucker said then. 'I want to know who was driving that car when it ran my wife down.'

'I don't know. I told you we had nothing to do with that. It was an accident, that's all. That's all I know.'

Tucker stood up slowly, reached down and picked up the automatic, released the safety, walked to Henemyer and stood over him, looking down. 'That's not good enough.'

'It's the truth. I'm telling you the truth.'

Tucker leaned over, pressed the muzzle of the gun against Henemyer's kneecap and squeezed the trigger. Henemyer screamed and his face went stark white as blood bubbled up through the hole in his pants. His leg lay flat, at an odd angle, stretched out oddly in front of him. Finally his voice came back, a raw whisper now. 'Jesus . . . what do you want from me? If you're gonna kill me, *do* it. Don't just . . .'

'Who was driving that car?'

'I don't know. I told you. I don't know.'

Tucker bent down again, pressed the automatic against Henemyer's other knee, and fired, a dry, snapping report in the cold room. Henemyer screamed again and slumped forward, half–conscious now, his upper body trembling, shaking the crib, the blood from his ruined knees spreading on the floor and meeting in a dark pool between his legs.

Tucker sat down on the chair again. When Henemyer looked up at him finally, his eyes staring and lips trembling, Tucker said, 'Who did it?'

'Brookshire. Brookshire drove the car and Pine was with him. I wasn't even there. I was in Washington . . .'

'Yeah, I know. You're innocent as hell.'

'I didn't have anything to do with it.'

'Who gave the order?'

'I don't know. Nobody. How would I know?'

Tucker moved over to him again, pressed the gun against his left elbow.

'Don't . . . Jesus . . . *please* . . .'

'Who gave the order?'

'Reser. Reser planned everything.' The words tumbled out now. 'Nobody knew the details except him . . . none of us knew till the last minute that we were going after Whittaker. I don't even think the President knew. I don't think he knows yet . . .' Henemyer's voice trailed off.

Tucker stood looking down at him. All the frustration and hopelessness, the heartbreak and hatred he'd kept inside himself for two months, bled through now and twisted his face.

'What about Applegate?' he said then.

Henemyer looked up now, his voice getting weaker and his lips bubbling out a disconnected chain of lies. But his eyes, bulging with fear, couldn't support the story. His eyes gave him away.

Tucker let it all sink in, read Henemyer's face carefully, like a printed poster. Then he pointed the gun straight down, at the spot where Henemyer's legs came together. He aimed carefully, his arm rigid from the shoulder to the wrist.

'This is for Applegate,' he said. And he fired twice.

CHAPTER FORTY–NINE

AT THREE O'CLOCK that afternoon, Nora Chester, leaving two customers at the grocery counter, went to answer her telephone.

'This is Roy. I need to talk to Deke.'

'He ain't here. He went down to the Legion hall over an hour ago.'

'Can you get in touch with him?'

'I could phone him, I reckon. When it's important the office girl can get him to the phone.'

164

'It's important,' Tucker said. 'Tell him I need him to drive me someplace. I'm at the Shell station on the county road just south of Waynesville.'

'That's Shep Luther's place. Deke knows him.'

'Tell him to bring that canvas bag I stuck in your upstairs closet. Not the little suitcase. Leave that there. Just the canvas bag. And tell him the quicker he gets here, the better.'

'You're not outside, are you? It must be zero.'

'No. I'm waiting in the office. Tell him to shake a leg.'

Half an hour later, Deke pulled in and stopped by the gas pumps in front of the Shell station. He waved to Shep Luther through the window as Tucker came out of the office and climbed into the front seat of the pickup beside him.

'Where's your car?' Deke said.

'In a ditch. How much gas you got in this thing?'

'Full tank. Close to it. Filled her up last evening.'

'I need a favour,' Tucker said. 'I need you to drive me to Charlotte. How far is it?'

'Sixty, seventy miles, I guess. If they ain't moved it.'

'Is there a back road way to get there?'

'That's the only route there is unless you want to drive to hell–and–gone out of your way. It's a hundred miles or better if you go northeast to pick up the four–lane.'

'Let's take the short way.'

The road was two–lane all the way, winding through hills and gullies and woods, some stretches rutted and slick with snow, others clean and clear for eight or ten miles at a time. It was a little after five o'clock when they entered the northern outskirts of Charlotte, and just after five–thirty, almost completely dark, when they turned into the four–lane approach to the airport.

'Just pull up in that lot there by the gate,' Tucker said. 'I'll walk myself in.'

'No trouble to drive you.'

'Thanks anyway, Deke. It's better if I get out here.'

When the truck slid to a stop, Tucker reached up behind the seat and dragged the canvas bag down on his lap. He turned to Deke and said, 'There's a dead man in your old house. He's tied up and shot upstairs in Thelma's room. Somebody will find him when he starts to stink and they'll find my car in the ravine not far away so there won't be any mystery about who shot him. Once the Asheville police get onto it, they'll know for certain it was me.'

'Jesus, Roy . . .'

'I had to do it, Deke. If he was alive now, I'd be dead. I'm just telling you all this so you'll stay away from the place. Outside of answering questions, there's no reason for you to be implicated any way at all. Nobody's gonna know you even saw me today unless you or Nora tells them. Or your friend at the Shell station.'

'We won't say nothing. Shep won't either.'

'I don't know for sure where I'm gonna be but I'll get in touch with you later if I can. But whether you hear from me or not, I left something for you in your upstairs closet. In that brown suitcase I hid there.'

'We got it locked up for you.'

'I don't want it. That's what I'm telling you. That's yours. Your's and Nora's. It's some money, money I earned and it's all in cash. I want you to have it.'

'We wouldn't want . . .'

'Don't argue with me, Deke. I don't have much time. I want you to take that money, wrap it up good, and hide it or bury it where nobody can find it. If anybody asks you, you don't know anything about anything. Then, when two or three years have gone by, you can take that money out of your sock and spend it for whatever you want.'

'I'm telling you Roy, there ain't nothing we need.'

'Just pretend you had a big insurance policy on Thelma. Just look at it like that.'

Inside the terminal, waiting in line to buy a ticket to Washington, Tucker saw the newspaper picture of Tom Reser. Just ahead of him in line, a girl in a red wool lumber jacket was reading the Charlotte *News-Sentinel*.

Tucker leaned closer and read the picture caption over her shoulder. In heavy type it said, **United Nations Speaker.** He strained to read the rest of the caption but the print was too small. Finally he said, 'Do you think I could look at your paper for a minute?'

The girl turned and looked at him. 'Are you talking to me?'

'I thought maybe you'd just let me look at the front page there for a second.'

Blank–faced, surrendering nothing, the girl said, 'I bought this paper about four minutes ago right over there at the news stand. They must have fifty or sixty more and they're all for sale.'

'I don't want to give up my place here in line. I'll be glad to pay you for it.' He took a quarter out of his pocket and offered it to her. 'You can have the money *and* the paper. I only need to see it for half a minute.'

She looked down at the quarter, then back at him. She shook her head and said, 'Talk about your one–track minds.' Then she handed him the paper.

'Thanks a lot.' He unfolded the paper, turned it over, located Reser's picture, and read the rest of the caption.

Thomas Reser will address the General Assembly in New York at three o'clock tomorrow afternoon prior to his departure for Saudi Arabia for meetings with Arab leaders.

When his turn came at the ticket desk, Tucker said, 'When's the next flight to New York?'

'Seven thirty–two. American flight 413. One stop. In Baltimore.'

'Okay.'

'Coach or first class?'

'Coach.' He took out Brookshire's credit card and placed it on the counter. Then, 'I changed my mind. Make it first class.'

'Will that be one–way or round trip?'

'One–way.' He set his canvas bag on the luggage scale. 'I hope you won't X–ray my bag. I've got some film and expensive camera equipment in there.'

'We only X-ray the carry–ons at this airport.'

'That's good.'

When he left the counter he bought a copy of the Charlotte paper at the news stand and threw all of it away but the front page. He carefully tore out Reser's picture then and dropped the remains of the page into a trash container. He folded the picture neatly and slipped it into his jacket pocket. When he looked up the girl in the red lumber jacket was standing a few feet away staring at him. She turned to the girl beside here, an overweight girl wearing a white toque over her dark hair, and said in a loud voice, 'I told you. He's a wacko. Eighteen carat wacko.'

CHAPTER FIFTY

THE COACH SECTION of the plane was filled. In first class, there were only five passengers. One of the stewardesses, a short, quick, blonde girl with a good smile, buckled herself into the seat beside Tucker as the plane took off.

'Boy, are we going to spoil you guys,' she said. 'Two stewardesses and five passengers. Jan and I love it when it's like this. We can booze and beefsteak our people to death. It's fun when you can really give the passengers some personal service. Sometimes the flights are so jammed it's all we can do to survive. Do you always fly first class?'

'I don't fly much. I flew first class once before.'

'On American?'

'I think it was Braniff.'

'They're good. I've got a friend from hostess training

who switched over to Braniff. Susan Bishop. She loves it. Where'd you fly to?'

'Chicago to Costa Rica.'

'Wow! That's a trip! Braniff doesn't go that whole route, do they?'

'I don't think so. I think I had to take some other airline from Honduras.'

'I'll bet you liked the flight, though, the Braniff part.'

'I don't remember it much to tell you the truth.'

'How long ago was it?'

'Second week in October. Around then.'

'Shame on you. That's only a little over two months ago.'

'It seems like longer.'

'I'll bet you ten to one it was a business trip,' she said. 'If it was a vacation you'd remember it. Am I right? Was it business?'

'I guess that's what you'd call it.'

'I knew it. That's ten thousand dollars you owe me.'

Tucker had two drinks before dinner. And a bottle of imported beer with his steak. After dessert and coffee, Patty offered him a cognac and a cigar.

'Perfect ending to the meal,' she said. 'That's what they tell me. A few sips of brandy and a few puffs on the old cigar–o.'

'No, thanks. I'm just fine. I had enough.'

When they began their descent for La Guardia, not till then, Tucker took out the folded picture of Reser, smoothed it carefully on his serving table, and studied the eyes, the straight mouth, the carefully trimmed moustache, tried to look at the picture objectively, tried to imagine what his impressions would be if this man were truly a stranger, someone he had never met or talked with or feared or hated.

Permanently ruled and defined by chance, guided all his life by impulse and instinct, Tucker tried, for those few moments, to be dispassionate, fully in control. But the centre would not hold. Other faces blurred through the printed image. Spiventa and Tagge and Applegate. And most persistently, Thelma.

Tucker realised suddenly that he was trembling. He gripped the arms of his seat till his muscles were hard and aching. Then he switched off the reading light, crumpled Reser's picture in his hand, and turned his face away from the aisle.

CHAPTER FIFTY–ONE

IT WAS NEARLY one o'clock in the morning when Tucker walked through the terminal at La Guardia, picked up his bag from the luggage carousel, and got into a taxi at the curb outside.

'Where's the United Nations Building?'

'Is that where you want to go?' the driver said.

'I just want to drive past there. Where is it?'

'First Avenue in the Forties.' He pulled out into the line of traffic. 'But there's nothing cooking there this time of night. Everything's shut up tight as a wad.'

'I don't need to stop. Just drive past.'

'Then what?'

'Then I have to find a hotel.'

Moving west toward the midtown tunnel, the driver speeding, darting from lane to lane in the light traffic, Tucker saw the dark mass of Manhattan, like a cruel, outsized Stonehenge, slowly loom up from the blackness across the river, its lighted windows sparkling coldly, burning dull glowing holes in the night. And on either side of the road, the startling acres of gravestones, mausoleums, and death monuments, picking up light from the cars racing by and from the colour–lit advertising signs, everything bleeding together in low–key colours, blood–red, burnt orange, purple and chrome yellow and mauve, on a ground of smoky rotting black, a lunatic's obscene painting of the road to hell.

'You live in New York?' the driver said.

'No. I've never been here before.'

'I've lived here all my life. It's a shit–house.'

'First time I've ever seen it.'

'It's a shit–house. Believe me.'

When they pulled out of the midtown tunnel and turned uptown on First Avenue, the driver said, 'It'll be right up ahead here on your right. They keep it all lit up. You can't miss it. They got to keep the lights on or else the rag-heads and the fruitcakes would be lobbing gasoline bombs over the fence all night long.'

He slowed down then and stopped at the curb. 'There she is. I remember when they signed the first papers. In some woods outside of San Francisco. No more fighting, they said. No more wars. 1945 that was. I was fresh out of the army and it all sounded good. But I had a buddy from Nebraska who said, "It's all horseshit. Mark my word. It's eighty proof horseshit." And he was right. There's been more fighting and killing in the last thirty years or so than all the rest of history put together. Only now it's nice and polite. Nobody declares war. It's like my wife's sister. She brags all the time that she's never had a divorce. What she don't say is she never bothered to get married. She just sacks in with anybody that asks her nice.'

Tucker stared at the squat General Assembly Building, round and heavy like a great white turtle, and behind it the dark glass-and-steel slab of the towering Secretariat, ghostlike, brooding and impregnable, structures without life or people, a moon landscape, the relic, it seemed, of a blueprint that hadn't worked, of a futurist city whose colonists had fled, blind and bleeding, back into whatever past they could salvage.

The driver took him to the Constable Hotel on Forty–

fourth Street, half a block east of Broadway. 'It ain't the Pierre but they tell me it's clean. And they won't charge you an arm and a leg. Only problem is if you see any black–assed hookers in the upstairs hall, run like a thief. 'Cause she'll probably be a guy with phoney boobs and his legs shaved. They'll cut out your liver and hand it to you for a dollar and a half.'

They put Tucker in a room on the fifth floor, at the front of the hotel, windows looking out on the street and another hotel across the way. The Mexican boy who carried his bag upstairs and unlocked the room said, 'Cold tonight. The most cold for this day of any time ever. Tomorrow more cold still.'

Tucker stood at the window in his overcoat looking down at the street. Finally he undressed, took a hot shower, got into bed and switched off the light.

The United Nations complex, cold and white, marble, glass and steel, walls and fences and searchlights, had burned itself into his brain. As he lay in bed with his eyes closed, it overpowered him and smothered him. Those dimensions, that sheer tonnage, crushed him, cut off his will and his energy and all his resources. Whatever stubborn, angry persistence had fuelled him and pushed him aboard the plane to New York, it dissolved now, melted and trickled away.

Wrapping the blankets around him, he pulled himself up in a ball the way he'd slept as a child, shivered in the cold darkness, and at last went to sleep.

CHAPTER FIFTY–TWO

THE COUNTERMAN WAS leaning against the back service cabinet by the coffee urn, reading the morning paper, grunting approval from time to time, and laughing. It was six o'clock in the morning, twelve degrees below zero outside, a raw cutting wind blowing up Sixth Avenue, rattling metal signs, and shaking the panes of glass and the metal grids of the shop windows.

In the coffee shop, northwest corner of Forty–fourth and Sixth, there were only two customers. Tucker on a centre stool, his coat collar turned up, drinking black coffee, and a very old woman, more than eighty, on the last stool against the wall, her coat pinned together and tied with bits of twine, a navy watch cap pulled down over her ears, a tattered discoloured rag of a muffler around her neck, and two paper shopping bags on the floor beside her, bulging with scraps of clothing, toys, magazines, and miscellaneous rags and found objects. On one bag was printed, *Bowery Savings Bank* and on the other, *Move Up To Ohrbachs*. Her eyes were pale and rheumy, her nose a painful reddish lavender, and her knobby hands were wrapped tight around her coffee mug soaking up the heat.

'You talk about your crazy bastards,' the counterman said, 'This guy Darby's got them all beat. I mean he don't care if school keeps or not. Listen to this: "We've got Disneyland and Disney World already. Now what we need is

Disney Washington, the biggest amusement park of all. It's a perfect set-up. The real work has been done already. We've got Humpty Dumpty in the White House, Snow White and her hundred mental dwarfs in the Senate. We've got Jesse James over at the I.R.S., Goofy runs the Treasury Department, and Dopey takes care of foreign policy.'"

The counterman slapped the folded paper down on the counter. 'Is *that* something? Has he got those lame brains nailed or has he?' He opened up a big carton of doughnuts and Danish pastry and began putting them on the shelves of a glass display-case.

'My cousin, Dave, had Darby in his cab once. Picked him up in the east Nineties, he said, and hauled him all the way down to Sardi's. Dave said he had him laughing so hard he damn near ran his hack up on that island in the middle of Park Avenue. Everybody says that Darby's been known to have a few. All those newspaper guys booze it up pretty good from what I hear. But you'd never guess it when you read the stuff he writes. I mean that guy's a *writer*. You don't have to be some college guy to tell that. He lays it right out square on the line. Even when he's got you laughing, you know he's giving you the straight poop. I mean he don't back off from anybody.

'You take Nixon, for example. Darby was taking pot-shots at him when everybody else still thought he was Little Boy Blue. And Lyndon Johnson. Darby said he had the instincts of a cattle rustler. And did you hear what he called Carter? *Mortimer Snerd*. A few days later he said he hadn't had any complaints from the White House but Edgar Bergen was suing him for slander.

'You know all those crap-hounds in Washington would like to hang him up by his ears if they could. But he doesn't care. He just keeps chopping away. Take Lindsay, for instance, that Barby Doll we had for a mayor. Darby saw through him from the start. When everybody else thought Lindsay was the man with the golden dick, Darby said he was a fake. Said Lindsay would give up politics in a minute if somebody offered him a job on *Hollywood*

Squares. And that's the way it turned out. The man was a lightweight. *Featherweight*, as a matter of fact. It'll take us fifty years to dig out of the mess he made. All because nobody listened to Darby.' He picked up Tucker's coffee cup and refilled it. 'You read any of those pieces he's been writing about Whittaker?'

'I don't live here. I just got in town, last night.'

'Well, you missed something. Darby's hot as hell about that subject. He says the whole story they've been handing us is a banana. Just like it was with Jack Kennedy and the black guy they knocked over down in Memphis . . . I can never think of his name . . .'

'King.'

'That's it. Martin Luther King. Anyway, Darby says the Whittaker thing is the biggest piece of cheese since Watergate. And I believe him. I mean you have to listen to guys like that. Everybody knows you get nothing straight from Washington. Or from Albany or City Hall either. I say thank God for guys like Darby who got the guts to stand up to the politicians and tell them they're feeding us a line of first–class bullshit.'

CHAPTER FIFTY–THREE

THREE HOURS LATER, in a twelve–room apartment over-looking Manhattan, on the top floor of the Waldorf Towers, four waiters in crisp jackets served breakfast.

The dining room was long, with a high ceiling, wide

windows on two walls, and glass doors with a terrace outside. The ceiling was soft white and the walls a pale creamy grey. Four paintings hung on the longest wall opposite the terrace doors, a Cézanne oil of Mont Ste Victoire, a Renoir family grouping – three women and a yellow–haired child, the very best seascape Rouault ever painted, and a bright Pissarro garden.

The table silver, the bowls and pitchers, *compotes* and candlesticks and butter dishes were heavy and ornate, the crystal Baccarat, the china delicate bone with a fine floral pattern.

The tables and chairs, the cabinets and sideboards were Louis Quatorze and the linen had been tediously hand-made sixty years before in St Brieuc. Thick Chinese rugs, blue and rose and ivory, muffled the footsteps of the waiters as they moved back and forth from the kitchen.

Fresh orange juice was served in silver bowls filled with crushed ice. Then grapefruit and orange segments, stewed pears and prunes and peaches; oatmeal, scones, thick slices of buttered toast, and bran muffins; platters of ham and sausage, kidneys and bacon and kippers; stacks of buttermilk cakes the size of silver dollars, scrambled eggs; coffee, tea, or cocoa, and a handsomely engraved silver pitcher of milk. At either end of the table, in silver buckets, magnums of unopened Dom Perignon.

The eight men at the table, seeming not to notice this truly awesome pageant of beautifully prepared food, sat stiffly erect in their chairs, talked quietly with each other, and ate very little.

At the head of the table, a thin and immaculate old man was sitting, skin like paper and delicate features, his hair dead–white and carefully trimmed above his high forehead, his wrists fragile, the veins purple and prominent on the backs of his hand, brown spots on his skin, his nails pink and buffed and polished.

At the old man's right sat Thomas Reser, wearing a dark blue suit, almost black, a pale blue shirt, and a dark tie with faint flecks of blue and red.

All the men around the table wore dark suits, blue or

grey, and conservative neckties. The youngest among them was fifty–seven, the oldest, the man at the head of the table, eighty–two. The median age was perhaps sixty–eight.

For all their wide range of physical characteristics, they resembled each other in some intangible way. There was a degree of finish, a patina, a uniformity of voice projection, a quiet presence, that stamped them as cultural kin. Shared backgrounds, shared values, a powerful sense of peership. They recognised each other in the simplest and most profound sense.

They *existed*, these men, élite and unanimous, like a sleek and powerful animal with eight heads, secure in its habitat, free to feed where it wished, wander where it chose, safe from poachers and trappers, permanently safe from everything, in truth, because the beast was not only shrewd and strong and resourceful, it was invisible.

At the end of the meal, when the food was taken away, the plates cleared, and the champagne opened at last, a tiny amount of the wine was poured into each crystal glass and the fragile birdman at the head of the table stood up.

In a scratchy voice barely audible across the room, he said, 'I speak for all of us, I am certain, when I commend Thomas Reser. We are in his debt and we will continue to be.' He turned his eyes to Reser. 'Most of us spend our lives in a private and anonymous way, not much noticed or applauded. Then there are a few who are *public* men, who are able to do critical work and sometimes change the shape of things. You're one of those men, Tom, and we are all grateful for it.'

As he took one sip from his glass and set it down, the other men around the table perfectly matched his movements.

CHAPTER FIFTY-FOUR

AT TEN-THIRTY in the morning, no relief from the acid
-edge, cutting cold, the air as motionless as though it
were frozen solid, the sky a brilliant cloudless blue, Tucker stood on the west side of First Avenue across the street
from the United Nations buildings.

At the curbs on both sides, heavy sawhorse barricades
had been set up and half a dozen police vans were parked
up and down the street.

Forty or fifty young people who looked like students
had started fires in three wire trash-containers and they
crowded as close as they could around them, bundled up,
the girls with long scarves and wool caps pulled down
over their ears, the boys wearing earmuffs or ski masks
and *yamulkes*. Stacked close by, leaning against the police
barricades, were dozens of picket signs, hand-lettered
sheets of poster board, stapled to five-foot lengths of wood
lath.

Tucker, his hands deep in his pockets, moved down
First Avenue. Other than the police vans, there were only
two vehicles parked on the street. Two long trucks, light
blue, and in neat white letters on their sides, WNET EDU-
CATIONAL TELEVISION.

As Tucker stopped at the rear of the second truck, a
young man stepped down out of the back carrying a metal
box, a blue and white wool cap on his head, wearing a
quilted blue jacket, the letters WNET in white across the

back. The jacket was zipped up high around his neck, a turtleneck sweater underneath it pulled up over his mouth and chin.

'What's going on?' Tucker said.

'What do you mean?' The man was closing the double back doors of the truck, locking them.

'I mean what's happening? All the police and everything.'

'Somebody's making a speech here this afternoon. There'll be two or three thousand people bumping heads out here in a couple of hours.' When he started across the street, Tucker walked beside him. 'Where you think you're going?'

'I hear they have public tours of these buildings.'

'Not today they don't. You picked the wrong time. *Nobody* gets in there today.'

They approached a narrow side gate in the wrought iron fence, and as the WNET man walked on through it, a uniformed guard stepped in front of Tucker.

'Back across the street, buddy. You think I'm standing out here for my health?'

'Somebody told me you have tours . . .'

'Sometimes we do. But not today.'

'I thought maybe since I'm from out of town . . .'

'You could be from the moon. It don't matter. You still have to stay on the other side of the street.'

'Maybe I could just . . .'

'Forget it, mister. We got no time to screw around today. Either you haul ass out of here or you'll end up sitting inside one of those police wagons wondering what hit you.'

Tucker walked west on Forty–sixth Street to Second Avenue, found a cab there, and told the driver, 'I want to go to the *New York Post* building.'

'That's only a few minutes' ride from here.'

'Good,' Tucker said. 'The quicker the better.'

'I mean you might as well walk it.'

'I don't want to walk it. I want to ride it. That's why I'm sitting here in your cab.'

179

'It ain't worth starting the meter for a two- or three-minute ride.'

Tucker leaned forward in the seat. 'Listen to me, you asshole. I've been in this town about twelve hours and I haven't seen anybody I like yet. Now either you drive me where I want to go or I'll lay you out in the snow and drive myself.'

When the taxi pulled up in front of the *Post* building, Tucker said, 'Hold your flag. I'll be back in a minute.'

'Nothing doing. I can't sit out here forever. I'm due at the garage in twenty minutes.'

'Plenty of time,' Tucker said. 'I'll be right back.'

He got out, crossed the sidewalk, and pushed through the revolving door of the building entrance. A uniformed guard sat at a desk just inside the door. 'What can I do for you?'

'I'm looking for a man named Darby.'

'Lots of people are.'

'What does that mean?'

'Just what it sounds like. Half the people in New York would like to sit down and chew the fat with Len Darby. But it ain't that easy to do.'

'This is important,' Tucker said.

'I didn't say it wasn't. I just said . . .'

'He works here, doesn't he?'

The guard nodded his head. 'He writes a piece for the paper three times a week. And he's got an office up in Editorial. But I only see him around here about twice a month on the average.'

'Then how can I talk to him?'

'All you can do is leave your name and phone number with me and I'll send it up to the secretary. Or you can call her on the phone yourself. Tell her what you want to see him about and she'll pass it along.'

When Tucker came back outside, the taxi was gone. He walked to Forty–fourth Street, then headed west to his hotel.

Upstairs in his room, he put a quarter in the television set. He sat on the edge of the bed watching the last part of a western film with Joel McCrea and Randolph Scott. Scott was dead at the end and McCrea was on his horse, riding slowly down from the mountains with two bullets in his chest. The time ran out then, the quarter dropped, and the set went black three minutes before the end of the picture.

Tucker sat for a long time staring at the mute square of the television screen. At last he got up, opened his canvas bag, and emptied it out on top of the bed.

CHAPTER FIFTY-FIVE

TWENTY MINUTES BEFORE Reser was scheduled to leave his hotel to be driven to the General Assembly, Milton Watson, chief of the security team that would take him there and stay with him all the way to Saudi Arabia and back, came into the sitting room where Reser was looking over his speech.

'Tunstall just called up from the lobby. There's a man named Stokely down there asking to see you.'

'Stokely?' Reser said. Then, very casually, 'Does Tunstall know him?'

'No. The guy wouldn't show any identification either. Just gave his name. Frank Stokely.'

'Does that ring a bell with you?'

'No. But Tunstall says the guy's not a crazy.'

Reser walked to the window, looked out, then turned back. 'All right. Tell Tunstall to bring him up. Put him in the room next door and let me know when he's there. I'll use the connecting door.'

'Don't worry. I'll be in the room.'

'No, you won't.'

'I'm sorry but I have orders, General Reser.'

'I just changed your orders.' He grinned then. 'You're losing your grip, Milt. Stokely's on our side. He's with the Bureau.'

'That's another world. We don't try to keep track of those cowboys. Why didn't he tell us?'

'Because he's a friend of mine. It's unofficial business. And I'd like it to stay unofficial. As far as you're concerned, Stokely wasn't here. Do we understand each other?'

'Yes, sir.'

Five minutes later, Reser opened the connecting door and went into the adjoining suite. Stokely was waiting there. Neither of them said anything till Reser had switched on the television set in the corner and turned it up to full volume. Then they stood face to face, their heads only a few inches apart, and spoke softly.

'What the hell are you doing here?'

'We've got a situation,' Stokely said. 'There wasn't any time and I didn't want to risk a phone call.'

'Henemyer?'

'He wasn't on the plane. And he wasn't on the later flights from Asheville. Have you heard from him?'

'No. What about the freak from Montreal?'

'I paid him off and sent him home. He's too hot to keep around.'

'Good,' Reser said. 'You did the right thing.'

'What about Henemyer? What do you want me to do?'

'Nothing. Forget about him.'

'If it had anything to do with that Tucker–Brookshire thing in Asheville . . .'

'What do you know about that?'

'Not much. Henemyer didn't make it very clear.'

'Then I'll make it clear. Then I want you to forget it. Brookshire's one of my men. He went a little psycho. That's all. He's under control now. Tucker's a cover name. There's no such animal.'

'I still don't see why Henemyer went to . . .'

'You don't have to see. But I'll tell you anyway. He went because I told him to. I was faking him out so we could set him up when he came back. He's a security risk. A serious one. I told you that. And that's all I told you. Don't try to connect him with anything because there's no connection to be made.'

'Yes, sir.'

'Forget you ever heard of Henemyer and Brookshire. That Asheville stuff never happened. You understand?'

'Yes, sir.' Then, 'What if Henemyer contacts me while you're out of the country.'

'He won't. I guarantee it.'

Ten minutes later, in the back seat of an armour–plated limousine, rolling downtown behind a police escort, secret service men on all sides, motorcycle officers surrounding his car, heading for the fortress–like security of the General Assembly Building, Reser was suddenly very afraid.

CHAPTER FIFTY–SIX

WITH NO SOLID plan in mind, no scheme, no device, with no key facts or information available to him, Tucker tried, nonetheless, to proceed by a timetable. At precisely two o'clock in the afternoon, he folded the Xerox pages, duplicates of the ones he had sent to Reser from Savannah and put them inside a nine–by–twelve manila envelope. He enclosed also the magazine clipping that Applegate had mailed to him in Chicago, all of the Brookshire identification papers he had been carrying, Henemyer's wallet with all his papers inside, and the tape cassette of Applegate's voice. Tucker sealed the envelope and wrote the name Len Darby on the outside.

Fifteen minutes later, he stood in front of the downstairs desk in the *New York Post* building, a different guard there, not the man Tucker had talked with earlier.

'I have something to leave for Mr Darby. If he's not here will you please see that his secretary gets it. It's important.'

'Yes, sir,' the guard said. 'I'll send it right up.'

From there Tucker walked to the United Nations Plaza, his hands in his pockets, his coat collar turned up, his face stinging in the white cold.

When he was still two blocks away from First Avenue, he could hear the chanting and shouting and screaming. He walked down to Forty–second and Third, then crossed to First so he could come out at the downtown end of the United Nations complex.

All motor traffic had been diverted from First Avenue. North at Fiftieth Street and south at Thirty–eighth, the street was barricaded.

As Tucker came to the end of Forty–second, in view of the General Assembly and the Secretariat, he saw a ragged and surging, disorganised battle taking place between Forty–fourth and Forty–sixth, spilling and straggling away noisily on all sides, young people carrying pro–Israeli signs in a clumsy struggle against an equally clumsy and screaming crowd of Arab sympathisers, riot police in the centre of the turmoil swinging night sticks, and mounted officers wheeling and charging back and forth through the crowd, their horses rearing and whinnying and kicking, eyes rolling back white in their heads.

Tucker shoved through the crowd on the sidewalk and went straight to the television truck. As he approached, he saw the man in a WNET jacket leave the truck and hurry across the street to the UN Plaza.

Tucker ran half a block south on First Avenue to the spot

where an empty police van was parked at the curb, unattended, no one in the front seat, no pedestrians close by. He stood near the van, watching the UN side gate. When the WNET man hurried out and headed for his truck again, Tucker waited till he was out of sight, just inside the back doors of the truck. Then he took one of the Vietcong grenades out of his pocket, pulled the pin, and rolled it under the police van. As he ran up the street toward the television truck, the van exploded behind him, the gas tank went quickly in a second explosion, and the van began to burn.

Tucker reached the rear end of the television truck just as the man inside was on his way out to see what had exploded. Tucker ran up the steep steps and pushed the man back inside.

'Wait a minute . . . what are you doing? Get the hell *out* of here.' He saw the pistol in Tucker's hand then and his voice dropped to a hoarse whisper. 'Jesus . . . don't . . .'

Tucker grabbed his collar, spun him around, and cracked him just behind the ear with the gun barrel. He caught the man as he slumped toward the floor and peeled off his jacket. Twisting out of his own coat, he put on the padded blue jacket, transferred the pistol and two grenades to the jacket pockets, and zipped the jacket up as high as it would go, the collar turned up over his chin and mouth. Taking the blue knit cap off the man's head, Tucker put it on and pulled it down to just above his eyes. Picking up a coil of electric cable then, he slung it over his shoulder, grabbed a metal electrician's box with his left hand, and climbing down from the truck, slammed the doors shut behind him.

Dodging between the horses and the shouting waves of people surging toward the burning van, Tucker struggled and fought his way across the street, angling toward the side entrance where two guards were watching the burning van, past them, on through the chaos in the gardens, and on in through the entrance of the building. The door guard, his attention focussed on the street, seeing the blue flash of the familiar jacket, let him pass without a second look.

Tucker turned left in the brightly lit foyer, walked along

the thick carpet, businesslike and sure of himself, through the tangle of dark–suited ministers and envoys who clogged the corridor and the open doorways leading down to the auditorium seats.

Ahead, on his right, Tucker saw a men's room door. He walked to the opposite wall of the corridor, set the coil of cable and the tool box down between a giant potted tree and the end of a long couch, recrossed the foyer, less crowded suddenly as more of the delegates disappeared down the aisles, stepped into the men's room, opened one of the cabinets, let himself in, and locked the door behind him.

CHAPTER FIFTY–SEVEN

IN HIS OPENING remarks to the General Assembly, Reser did not follow his prepared speech. After being introduced, after the applause had died down, he said, 'Anyone who questions the wisdom of the decisions I will announce here today should walk outside and observe carefully what's going on in the streets. There you will see the senseless violence, the mindless conflicts, that threaten all of us at this moment in history. The incipient anarchy that we see around us is a weapon against all civilised communities, against all forms of government. Rejection of authority is the most dangerous weapon of all, more than rockets or nuclear submarines or neutron bombs. That attitude, which is becoming an international virus, is the single element in contemporary life that we have most to fear, all of us, whether we are citizens of a major world power or of the newest emerging nation.'

Reser's words, quiet and persuasive, purred out of loudspeakers all through the corridors and offices and anterooms of the United Nations buildings. In the gentlemen's lounge where Tucker waited, Reser was an intimate presence.

The fact of that voice was critical to Tucker. It anchored Reser, located and targeted him, just at the bottom of the assembly hall, where the aisles converge, on the soft–lighted and isolated central podium. As long as that measured speech continued, Tucker could wait. When it stopped, the waiting would be over.

So the voice as a signal was critical. But the words meant nothing to Tucker. As his ears monitored the sounds his mind was far off, in another level of consciousness altogether, full concentration on a series of memory pictures, as crisp and beautiful as projected film, himself and Thelma in the house by the ocean in Costa Rica, on the terrace, in the garden, in the bedroom, eating, sleeping, drinking, talking and laughing.

There was no sadness in it. He was past that. It was a physical thing, a feast for his eyes and his senses, like turning pages filled with smiling summer scenes, all clear skies and brilliant savage flowers and no possible end to it ever.

CHAPTER FIFTY–EIGHT

RESER STOOD, TRIM and erect, his hands gripping the edges of the speaker's stand; he paused for a long moment and studied the faces in the crowded auditorium. Then he sliced through into the final paragraphs of his speech.

'To those who say that armament is a preparation for war, we say that judicious, balanced armament is an assurance of peace. To those who say we are abandoning the courageous people of Israel, we say we are supporting our Jewish friends, defending them, as we always have.

'We believe that the surest way to peace in the Middle East is for all the nations, Arab and Israeli alike, to be fully armed for their own defence. Defence. That is the key word. The arms programme I have described to you, the programme we will offer to the Arab leaders is designed for peace, not war.

'We are convinced . . . a nation that is confident in its ability to defend itself will not be an aggressive nation. Fully armed peoples have respect for themselves and respect for their neighbours. And that respect is surely a foundation stone for the tower of peace we are all so desperately anxious to build.'

Reser paused again, his eyes focused on some spot half–way back in the auditorium; he stood immobile while the silence crackled around him. Then, in a very quiet voice, scarcely more than a husky whisper, 'As a man who has spent his entire adult life, more than forty years, in public service, I can only say that the honour of this moment makes all those years seem like time well spent.'

He dropped his eyes then and the auditorium shook with applause. The delegates and the carefully screened guests and the members of the press all stood and cheered. No one moved to leave. Each person stood at his seat applauding and cheering.

Resser stood immobile, his arms at his sides, looking out at the audience, a grave and humble expression on his face.

Suddenly then, in the empty centre aisle, he saw a man in a bright blue jacket walking deliberately toward him from the back of the assembly. Half-way down the aisle, un-noticed by the still-cheering crowd, the man began to run. And Reser knew it was Tucker.

As Reser spun away from the rostrum and ran toward the exit door at the front of the hall behind the speaker's platform, Tucker threw the first grenade. It lobbed over Reser's head, exploded twenty feet past him and broke his left leg with a spray of shrapnel.

When the grenade exploded and Reser went down, when Tucker clubbed off a guard who had jumped on his back, when Watson raced up the aisle with his revolver out and fell with a bullet in his shoulder, the auditorium exploded in panic. Screams and shouts, wrestling and shoving. And swearing in forty languages. Men climbing over seats, climbing over each other, clogging the aisles, fighting for the emergency exits, or pushing up the aisles towards the foyer.

Apart from Watson, only one other security man had seen Tucker throw the grenade. Punching and elbowing his way through the crowd, vaulting over rows of seats, he got close enough to burn one close-up bullet into Tuc-ker's side before the crowd shoved him backward to the floor and trampled over him as they fought their way up the aisle.

Tucker, nearing the bottom of the aisle now, running, shoving, and dodging, blood spurting from his side, ran up the steps to the speaker's platform. With one last thrust of savage energy, he wrestled and clawed his way through to Reser, people falling back when they saw the grenade in his hand, surging back against the security men, blocking their line of fire.

Dragging his shattered leg, pale from fright and loss of blood, Reser had managed to pull himself up on his good knee. Spotting him there like a praying cripple, Tucker ran straight at him, dived on him, and drove him backward to the floor. With one knee on his chest, Tucker pried Reser's mouth open, shoved a grenade inside and pushed it deep back in his throat. Then as three men grabbed Tucker's shoulders and wrestled him backward, he pulled the pin and let himself be jerked and pummelled away. And he saw Reser's head blow apart.

The last thing Tucker saw before they shot him, his last conscious image, was Reser's headless body jerking and twitching across the floor gushing black blood on the carpet. The very last life–sound that came out of Tucker's throat was a hoarse cry of triumph.

STAR BOOKS BESTSELLERS

THRILLERS

OUTRAGE	*Henry Denker*	£1.95 ☐
FLIGHT 902 IS DOWN	*H Fisherman &*	£1.95 ☐
	B. Schiff	
TRAITOR'S EXIT	*John Gardner*	£1.60 ☐
ATOM BOMB ANGEL	*Peter James*	£1.95 ☐
HAMMERED GOLD	*W.O. Johnson*	£1.95 ☐
DEBT OF HONOUR	*Adam Kennedy*	£1.95 ☐
THE FIRST DEADLY SIN	*Laurence Sanders*	£2.60 ☐
KING OF MONEY	*Jeremy Scott*	£1.95 ☐
DOG SOLDIERS	*Robert Stone*	£1.95 ☐

CHILLERS

SLUGS	*Shaun Hutson*	£1.60 ☐
THE SENTINEL	*Jeffrey Konvitz*	£1.65 ☐
OUIJA	*Andrew Laurance*	£1.50 ☐
HALLOWEEN III	*Jack Martin*	£1.80 ☐
PLAGUE	*Graham Masterton*	£1.80 ☐
MANITOU	*Graham Masterton*	£1.50 ☐
SATAN'S LOVE CHILD	*Brian McNaughton*	£1.35 ☐
DEAD AND BURIED	*Chelsea Quinn Yarbo*	£1.75 ☐

STAR Books are obtainable from many booksellers and newsagents. If you have any difficulty tick the titles you want and fill in the form below.

Name_____

Address_____

_____

Send to: Star Books Cash Sales, P.O. Box 11, Falmouth, Cornwall. TR10 9EN.

Please send a cheque or postal order to the value of the cover price plus:
UK: 45p for the first book, 20p for the second book and 14p for each additional book ordered to the maximum charge of £1.63.

BFPO and EIRE: 45p for the first book, 20p for the second book, 14p per copy for the next 7 books, thereafter 8p per book.

OVERSEAS: 75p for the first book and 21p per copy for each additional book.

While every effort is made to keep prices low, it is sometimes necessary to increase prices at short notice. Star Books reserve the right to show new retail prices on covers which may differ from those advertised in the text or elsewhere.

STAR BOOKS BESTSELLERS

FICTION

WAR BRIDES	*Lois Battle*	£2.50 ☐
AGAINST ALL GODS	*Ashley Carter*	£1.95 ☐
THE STUD	*Jackie Collins*	£1.75 ☐
SLINKY JANE	*Catherine Cookson*	£1.35 ☐
THE OFFICERS' WIVES	*Thomas Fleming*	£2.75 ☐
THE CARDINAL SINS	*Andrew M. Greeley*	£1.95 ☐
WHISPERS	*Dean R. Koontz*	£1.95 ☐
LOVE BITES	*Molly Parkin*	£1.60 ☐
GHOSTS OF AFRICA	*William Stevenson*	£1.95 ☐

NON-FICTION

BLIND AMBITION	*John Dean*	£1.50 ☐
DEATH TRIALS	*Elwyn Jones*	£1.25 ☐
A WOMAN SPEAKS	*Anaïs Nin*	£1.60 ☐
I CAN HELP YOUR GAME	*Lee Trevino*	£1.60 ☐
TODAY'S THE DAY	*Jeremy Beadle*	£2.95 ☐

BIOGRAPHY

IT'S A FUNNY GAME	*Brian Johnston*	£1.95 ☐
WOODY ALLEN	*Gerald McKnight*	£1.75 ☐
PRINCESS GRACE	*Gwen Robyns*	£1.75 ☐
STEVE OVETT	*Simon Turnbull*	£1.80 ☐
EDDIE: MY LIFE, MY LOVES	*Eddie Fisher*	£2.50 ☐

STAR Books are obtainable from many booksellers and newsagents. If you have any difficulty tick the titles you want and fill in the form below.

Name_____

Address_____

_____

Send to: Star Books Cash Sales, P.O. Box 11, Falmouth, Cornwall. TR10 9EN.

Please send a cheque or postal order to the value of the cover price plus:
UK: 45p for the first book, 20p for the second book and 14p for each additional book ordered to the maximum charge of £1.63.

BFPO and EIRE: 45p for the first book, 20p for the second book, 14p per copy for the next 7 books, thereafter 8p per book.

OVERSEAS: 75p for the first book and 21p per copy for each additional book.

While every effort is made to keep prices low, it is sometimes necessary to increase prices at short notice. Star Books reserve the right to show new retail prices on covers which may differ from those advertised in the text or elsewhere.